E-mail to Chief Max Zirinsky, Courage Bay Police Department
From Casey Guthrie, motorcycle patrol officer

Chief Zirinsky—

I called in last night to give the investigators a heads-up about yesterday's pileup on the Pacific Coast Highway, but I wanted to make sure you got this in writing.

There was something really weird about that crash.

First thing that happens, a sedan in the northbound lane suddenly explodes and bursts into flames. Then the tractor-trailer rig flips trying to avoid the burning vehicle. That sets off a chain reaction and the rest you know about. Strange thing is, only moments later, a second blast of flames shoots out of the sedan. I can buy one explosion from the fuel tank, but two?

I also thought you'd like to know that Courage Bay's emergency services were in top form. Somebody should send a note to the hospital's chief of staff about Jackie Kellison. Kellison's an E.R. nurse whose car was totaled in the pileup. She was amazing to watch. The minute she crawled out of her car, she started treating the other victims. I'd bet more than one person owes her for saving their life.

I'm off for the next four, but call me on my cell if any of the guys on the investigative team need more info about the explosion.

Casey

About the Author

CODE RED

C.J. CARMICHAEL

gave up the exciting, glamorous life of income tax forms and double entry bookkeeping when she sold her first book to Harlequin Superromance in 1998. Though most of her time is spent on her first love, Superromances, she has also written one Intrigue, an online novella for eHarlequin and several books for Harlequin's continuity series. A past RITA® Award nominee for Best Long Contemporary Series, as well as a *Romantic Times* nominee for career achievement in romantic suspense, C.J. lives in Calgary, Alberta, where she and her husband and their two daughters enjoy hiking and skiing—and just looking at!—the Rocky Mountains.

CODE RED

C.J. CARMICHAEL

NEXT OF KIN

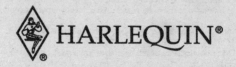

HARLEQUIN®

TORONTO • NEW YORK • LONDON
AMSTERDAM • PARIS • SYDNEY • HAMBURG
STOCKHOLM • ATHENS • TOKYO • MILAN • MADRID
PRAGUE • WARSAW • BUDAPEST • AUCKLAND

HARLEQUIN BOOKS
225 Duncan Mill Road, Don Mills,
Ontario, Canada M3B 3K9

ISBN 0-373-61286-9

NEXT OF KIN

Copyright © 2004 by Harlequin Books S.A.

C.J. Carmichael is acknowledged as the author of this work

www.eHarlequin.com

Printed in U.S.A.

Dear Reader,

In cities all over North America, traffic accidents are a tragic fact of everyday life. People are injured, sometimes they die, and many lives are changed forever. But can good ever come from bad?

While writing this book, I grappled with this question, as well as with two of the most daring characters I have ever written about. Motorcycle cop Casey Guthrie and emergency room nurse Jackie Kellison are people of strong convictions. When it comes to doing the right thing, they're not afraid to put their careers—or their lives—on the line. When it comes to her heart, however, Jackie is much more protective.

I hope you enjoy *Next of Kin* and the entire exciting CODE RED series. I'd love to hear what you think about this or any of my other books. Send mail to my Canadian address: #1754-246 Stewart Green, S.W., Calgary, Alberta, Canada T3H 3C8. Or contact me through my Web site (don't forget to enter my contest for free books while you're there).

Sincerely,

C.J. Carmichael
www.cjcarmichael.com

Acknowledgments

It was an honor to be asked to work on the Code Red project. I appreciate all the hard work that went into this exciting series at Harlequin—in particular the discerning eyes and good judgment of Marsha Zinberg and Margaret Learn. To all the Code Red authors, who answer e-mail so promptly and with such good nature, it's been a great experience!

Thanks to Sergeant W. R. Martin for answering all my questions (and questions, and questions!) so thoroughly and patiently.

Linda Prenioslo—always the best, the warmest of neighbors—thanks for sharing your medical expertise.

To my friend and fellow author, Eileen Coughlan, who helped me wrestle with this plot—I appreciate so much the times we get together and share our passion for writing.

And finally, to my husband, Mike, who brainstormed this book with me for the entire car trip from Calgary to Edmonton—this one's for you!

PROLOGUE

HIDDEN IN THE SHADOW of a stucco pillar outside the Super Value Mall on the southeastern outskirts of Courage Bay, a diminutive blonde clutched a baby to her chest and scrutinized the passing cars. A mini-van wheeled by, but she couldn't see in the tinted windows. Next, a two-seater Jeep zipped by, then a convertible.

The baby was getting heavy in her arms and the diaper bag kept sliding off her narrow shoulder. She eyed the vehicles with increasing desperation. This hadn't been part of the plan. Could she pull it off? The only answer she could come up with was that she had to. He'd slashed her tires, taken the money. What else could she do?

Finally she spotted a silver-gray Taurus wagon with an infant car seat in the back. The driver was an elderly woman—a grandma, maybe? The vehicle nosed into a parking place an aisle over from where the blonde was standing.

Impatiently she waited as the driver turned off her car and carefully stowed her sunglasses in a leather case on the dashboard. Finally the driver's door opened and the lady emerged. She opened the cargo door and pulled out a slick, fold-up stroller.

Hey, I should get one of those. As soon as the blonde had the thought, she gave herself a mental kick. *As if.* What was she thinking? She was not keeping this baby, no way…though at two months, it was awfully cute.

With the stroller set up beside her, the lady reached into the rear seat and pulled out a bundle in several blue blankets. She fussed some more, re-turned one of the blankets to the car, then finally closed the door and locked it, slipping the keys into the front pocket of her lightweight jacket.

It was October in Southern California. The jacket and the blankets weren't exactly necessary. The day was sunny and warm, with a gentle breeze coming off the ocean. Fortunately it wasn't raining, which it could easily do at this time of year. Still waiting, she shifted the baby to her other hip. Her heart pounded so loudly now, it was all she could hear.

The moment the lady pushed the stroller into the mall, the blonde stepped out from behind the pillar and followed. Through the heavy glass doors, past a small shoe-repair shop, a chain drugstore, a beauty salon. The lady with the stroller turned left at a kiosk selling hemp jewelry and soon reached her destina-tion: Baby Gap.

She went straight to the sales rack, flipping through the tiny items and selecting a few. Observ-ing from a safe distance, the blonde had to force her-self not to think about baby outfits herself.

Ten minutes later, with a dark blue plastic bag looped over one of the stroller handles, the lady emerged from the store. This time she stopped at a women's wear shop and again headed directly for the discount racks. Spotting a sweater she liked, she shrugged out of her jacket and threw it over the back of the stroller.

The blonde stiffened, spotting her chance. Trying to appear nonchalant, she strolled into the lady's line of vision and pretended to be interested in a row of T-shirts next to the stroller. She slid in as close as she dared, then brushed a hand over the jacket. The first pocket held nothing but a folded tissue.

Frantically she searched the second pocket. In front of her, the lady was admiring herself in a mirror. She swiveled, then smiled at the baby in the stroller. "What do you think, darling? Should Grandma buy this sweater?"

The blonde froze, certain that she was about to be busted. But a saleswoman walked between them at that moment.

"Oh, yes!" the saleswoman exclaimed with fake enthusiasm. "That pink really brings out the color in your cheeks."

The blonde felt the hard metal of the car key chain and closed her fingers around it. She eased her hand out of the jacket and into the pocket of her jeans. Then she turned around and left the store.

Five minutes later she was at the silver wagon, doing up the buckles of the infant car seat. "You be good back here, okay?"

The little one was due for a bottle, but that would have to wait. With luck, once the car was moving, the baby would be lulled to sleep. In the meantime, she dug a mirror from her purse and propped it up with a blanket in front of the child's face. She smiled as the infant gazed intently at the reflection.

"Look at the pretty baby," she cooed as she tossed the diaper bag on the floor between the car carrier and the back of the passenger seat. After a few quick adjustments to the driver's seat and the rearview mirror, she was ready to go. Cautiously she drove out of the mall with racing heart and damp palms. That poor grandma was in for a nasty surprise when she finished shopping, but it wasn't *her* fault.

Only one man could help them now, and he lived in one of the rich neighborhoods at the other end of town. Following the roadway signs carefully—this was not the time to make a stupid mistake with directions—she was soon heading north on the Pacific Coast Highway.

CHAPTER ONE

OFFICER CASEY GUTHRIE settled on the seat of his BMW motorcycle, then kicked back the side stand. He waited patiently while the driver of the black Lexus put away his license and vehicle registration papers. God, it was a great day. He relished the warmth of the late-afternoon sun on his head and shoulders.

His dayshift was over—this ticket had been the last. After a quick shower and nap at home, he'd be heading out to party. Some guys he'd gone to the academy with were in town and wanted to hit a few bars.

The man in the Lexus shot him a dark look as he shoulder-checked before merging once more into traffic. The irate businessman was going to be even later for his meeting than he'd anticipated. Maybe next time he'd leave a few minutes early and avoid the need to rush.

But probably not.

Casey revved his BMW, then shot off behind the Lexus, following the guy for a few minutes as a mild warning to keep that speed under control. After ten minutes he pulled a U-turn at an uncontrolled intersection and headed back the way he'd come, toward the station.

That last ticket had made him a little late, so Casey decided to hit the highway rather than navigate the slower inner-city roads. As he approached the feeder lanes, he carefully shoulder-checked. Two blondes in a white convertible sped by. One waved. The other blew a kiss. Too bad he'd turned off his radar. Pulling those two over would have been fun. He might have ended up with a date for tonight.

With a sigh of regret, he merged onto the highway. The sad truth was, he was really looking forward to his shower and nap more than the night on the town with the boys. He'd probably be happier spending the evening with his big brother, Adam, and his fiancée, Faith. Since hooking up with the bright defense attorney, the ever-serious chief of detectives had lightened up considerably. Last time they'd had a meal together, Adam hadn't mentioned a word about Casey needing to think about his future.

Paradoxically, Casey had begun to dwell on that very topic. For the past ten years, getting paid to zip around the pretty oceanside city of Courage Bay on a motorcycle all day had seemed too good to be true. But a cop couldn't stay on motorcycle patrol forever. Where did he want to be in ten years when he was forty?

The speed limit on the highway was sixty miles an hour, so Casey opened the throttle, shooting ahead of the dawdling Corolla in front of him. Compelled by the beauty of the day, he had to fight a sudden urge to do a little speeding himself. The ocean sprawled lazily on his left, and though it was October, the beach was dotted with sunbathers and swimmers.

Was there any finer place on earth than Courage Bay, California? The urge to get home grew stronger. He forced himself to slow down a fraction. He'd be there soon enough.

In his rearview mirror he spotted a pretty brunette in a Mazda convertible coming up in the left lane. Her hair was tied back and she wore sunglasses. Her lips were moving, though she was alone in the car. Probably singing along to the radio. She looked happy.

She was also speeding. She shot right past him, but must have caught sight of his bike and the insignia on the side, because a second later her brake lights flashed once, and then again.

Raising a hand to the side of his helmet, he met her gaze in her rearview mirror and gave her a mock salute. *I'm off duty, ma'am. Lucky for you.*

He slowed even further and soon she was lost in the lines of traffic ahead of him. Unlike the two blondes, whom he'd immediately forgotten, this brunette stuck in his mind.

RELIEVED THAT HE HADN'T signaled her to pull over, Jackie Kellison smiled at the reflection of the good-looking motorcycle policeman in her rearview mirror. She still had half an hour before her shift at Courage Bay Hospital's ER started, so she'd had no reason to exceed the speed limit.

But there was something about this day that made her feel a little reckless. The weather so perfect, the ocean so calm, the air so sweet. The wind must be blowing in the right direction, because not a wisp of smog spoiled the vivid blues of sky and water.

She checked the mirror again. The motorcycle cop was now several vehicles behind her. She felt mildly disappointed. He was cute, and surely she hadn't imagined the playful grin he'd directed toward her when she'd automatically pumped on her brakes. Maybe it would have been fun to be ticketed by him.

Jackie, Jackie, Jackie, she admonished herself. Her life really was dull if she imagined getting a traffic citation would be fun.

Leaning forward, she turned the radio volume higher and resumed singing to the Dixie Chicks' latest single. Yes, the truth was her life *was* extremely dull. She couldn't recall the last time she'd done anything just because she thought it would be fun. Even speeding was rashly uncharacteristic of her these days.

Maybe the old Jackie was coming back?

No, not quite. But a modified version, someone stronger…and wiser. Michael had said she'd heal eventually, and bless his kind, patient soul, he'd been right.

She didn't credit only Michael, gifted therapist that he was, with her mental recovery, though. She could never have managed without the support of her brothers. Since her grandfather's death when they were all kids, Robert—or Kell, as everyone called him—and Nate had been her only family and, as a result, the three of them were very thick.

They'd been almost as devastated as her when Andrew... But no. She wouldn't think of him now. She would just enjoy the rest of her drive to work and maybe even fantasize a little about the cute cop on that wicked motorcycle.

THE BABY IN THE BACK SEAT was crying now. Damn. She should have taken the time to warm a bottle at the mall. What was she going to do? Traffic was so heavy, she couldn't pull over to the side. Could she somehow get a bottle from the diaper bag while she was driving?

Cautiously, the blonde reached her right arm back toward the bag. She caught the strap and managed to pull it forward a few inches until it jammed between the infant carrier and the front passenger seat.

Oh, hell. Couldn't anything go right today?

"It's okay, sweetie. I'll get you something to eat." The constant wailing was giving her a headache. She groped for the bag's zipper, trying to remember into which compartment she'd packed the bottle.

In the instant she had her eyes off the road, the air suddenly shook with a huge explosion. The car in front of her burst into flames. She screamed and grabbed onto the steering wheel with all her might.

Oh, God, no. The burning car careened into the next lane, cutting off a huge tractor-trailer rig that had been passing them on the left-hand side. The rig driver hit his brakes, but couldn't avoid the collision. She heard the most awful noise of tires screeching on pavement, metal grinding on metal. The trailer zigzagged beside her—it was going to overturn!

She was trapped by traffic on all sides. There was nowhere for her to escape.

Help me. Help me. Oh, God...dear God...

AN EXPLOSION OF SOUND cut off Jackie's effort at positive thinking. Crashing metal, screeching tires, shattering glass. Several cars ahead of her, a huge tractor-trailer rig overturned, amid a cloud of thick black smoke. As her Mazda rushed toward the bumper of the vehicle in front of her, she slammed on her brakes. There was no way to prevent the crash. She braced herself for impact.

"Oh!" Her airbag deployed, knocking the breath from her lungs. She'd hit the car in front of her, and less than a second later felt an impact from the rear as the vehicle behind her joined the pileup.

I've had a car crash! For the few seconds that she couldn't breathe, she wondered if she was going to make it. Was this what she had suffered through the last two years of her life for? To die in a traffic accident?

CHAPTER TWO

THE RED MAZDA had been out of sight for over a minute when Casey crested a hill on the highway and spotted it again amid the steady traffic ahead. He wondered where the pretty brunette was off to in such a hurry. Or maybe she was just speeding because she had a great car and it was a lovely day and she was happy to be alive. Though he was paid to control the speed on the public roadways, Casey could relate only too well.

And then with a flash of light and boom of an explosion, everything about the day changed. Flames shot from a car even farther ahead on the road.

Casey swore as he automatically reached for his radio. At that instant, a tractor-trailer unit started to weave across two lanes of the highway, the driver trying desperately to avoid the out-of-control burning vehicle.

With a quick maneuver, Casey pulled over to the shoulder, watching helplessly as the rig zigzagged across several lanes of traffic. In a chain reaction, the vehicles behind the rig began to smash into each other, one after the other, filling the air with the smell of burning rubber and the horrific noise of crashing metal and shattering glass.

The tractor-trailer finally stopped moving, settling across the highway, then tipping inward and over, crushing whatever had been in the right-hand lane next to it. The rig landed lengthwise across the highway, blocking two northbound lanes and crossing the short median strip to settle over one southbound lane, too. Automobiles in both directions crashed into each other, creating the most massive pileup he'd ever witnessed.

"Ten forty-five on Pacific Coast Highway heading north. Repeat, 10-45 on PCH. At least twenty vehicles, probably more…"

He stopped to catch his breath, realizing that he was in a mild state of shock. This one had come a little too close to home. If he'd been going just a bit faster…

"We've got a huge pileup blocking most, if not all, south- and northbound lanes."

The dispatcher asked him to estimate the location.

"About five miles south of Courage Bay Hospital." *Which is damn lucky, since a lot of these unfortunate folk are going to require medical help, fast.* "We'll need everything you can get us. Backup, ambulances…"

He paused as he noticed a second blast of flames come from the burning vehicle. He frowned, wondering what could have caused two explosions in the same car. Not that it would matter to the poor driver, who had probably been incinerated with that first blast.

"What just happened?" the dispatcher asked.

Casey relayed the bare facts, then reiterated the need for help, as soon as possible. As he spoke he wove his motorbike between stopped vehicles, working his way up to the collision. Ahead, in the burning sedan, flames reached out of the gaping windows as if grasping for the sky. After a few moments the fire tapered down again.

If the second explosion had been the fuel tank, then what had caused the initial blaze? Casey made a note to discuss the anomaly with whoever headed up the investigation team later. Likely the poor devils would be here until late tonight, gathering statements from witnesses as well as physical evidence from the road and the vehicles involved in the collision.

Though he hated the carnage of serious traffic accidents, Casey had always enjoyed the process of collision reconstruction. It was like detective work, really, requiring a meticulous gathering of evidence from witnesses and from the accident scene itself.

At some point tonight, officers would carefully examine the road for skid marks, scrapes, gouges, liquid spills. They'd photograph the scene, take precise measurements with a transit, conduct a preliminary inspection of the vehicles involved. All this information would enable the officer in charge of the investigation to stand up in court and explain accurately how the accident had happened and why.

All very cool, fascinating stuff.

But right now, Casey's job was the opposite of

cool. His first concern was public safety. He circled the area with warning flares, shaking his head at the extensive damage. Somehow he had to clear a path through this mess for the emergency vehicles. The far southbound lane was probably his best bet. He began directing those drivers whose cars were still capable of moving to the side of the road.

FINALLY, JACKIE WAS ABLE to catch her breath. She flexed her hands, wiggled her toes, and decided she was okay. Her neck ached a little, but that was all. Around her the cacophony of the accident had died down. In the sudden silence she heard people calling for help.

How many drivers and passengers had been injured?

She scrambled for the cell phone she kept in her glove compartment for emergencies and dialed 9-1-1. The dispatcher seemed already aware of the incident, but still asked several questions. Ignoring a painful protest from her neck muscles, Jackie reached under the passenger seat for her first-aid kit.

After being assured that help was on its way, she disconnected her call and dropped the phone. She had to get out of here to see if she could help. She grasped the door handle, but even with a good shove from her shoulder, couldn't get the door to budge. Her beautiful new convertible was totally wrecked.

On shaky legs she stood on her seat. Before coming to a final stop, the tractor-trailer rig had crossed the center-line, and traffic now stood at a complete halt in both directions on the highway.

God give me strength, she prayed as she climbed out the open roof. The awful sounds of crying and moaning and entreaties for help were everywhere now. She hardly knew where to turn.

The bright sun suddenly seemed an abomination. She'd never seen such devastation firsthand. In front of her was a tangle of metal and shattered glass. Just ahead of the overturned rig, a sedan burned wildly. Had the occupants made it out before the blast? She prayed so.

"Please, help me! My son is bleeding badly!"

The woman in the car in front of Jackie's had managed to open the driver's side window and was waving at Jackie. She sprang into action, scrambling over the torn metal of the Mazda's hood, then jumping down to the pavement and racing to the woman's aid.

"Where is he bleeding?" Jackie pulled on a pair of disposable latex gloves as she spoke.

"His arm."

Peering in the passenger window, she saw a boy of about fifteen or sixteen strapped into the seat. He was shifting restlessly, and bright red blood spurted from a cut artery in his upper arm.

Jackie grasped the door handle and tugged. "How about you?" she asked the mother. "Are you all right?"

"I'm okay. Just please, please, look after Brayden."

Jackie wasn't convinced. The woman had the beginnings of a bruise on her forehead. But she was conscious and talking and able to move. That made the son the priority right now.

The door jammed. She put a foot against the car and tugged with all her might. To her amazement, the door fell to the road. She leaned in for a closer look at the boy. His respirations were rapid and shallow.

"Hi there, Brayden. That's quite a nasty cut you have." She was glad to see his eyelids flutter when she spoke to him. Pulling off her cardigan, she used it to stem the flow of blood. His mother was at Jackie's side now, having extracted herself from the car.

"Is he going to be okay?"

"I think so." She hadn't had a chance to inspect for other injuries yet. She had thick absorbent pads and bandages in her kit and did her best to dress the wound. As she worked, she spoke calmly to the mother.

"We need to stop the flow of blood until help arrives." The matronly woman stared at her blankly, probably in mild shock.

"Here." Jackie took one of the woman's hands and placed it over the bandaged wound. "You need to apply firm, direct pressure right here. Can you do that?"

The woman nodded.

"Good. Help will be here soon and your son will be fine. Be strong." She clasped a hand on the woman's shoulder, then slipped on her stethoscope to continue her examination.

The boy's pulse was fast, but thready. She took one of his hands and squeezed it gently. "Can you hear me, Brayden? If you're too tired to talk, then squeeze my fingers."

Nothing. He was probably in shock, too.

"Do you have anything warm in your van?" she asked the mother.

"A sleeping bag from my son's sleep-over last weekend."

"Great. Can you get it?" She kept pressure on the wound and managed to recline the boy's seat to a supine position while the mother found the sleeping bag.

"Here it is."

"Keep him warm," she told the woman, then, noticing that she had started to shake, added, "Actually, why don't you crawl under that sleeping bag with him?"

Moving on, she saw several people with minor injuries: a man with an obviously fractured arm, a woman with superficial abrasions on her face. They could wait.

The motorcycle cop who'd let her go earlier had cordoned off the accident site and was trying to clear a lane for the emergency vehicles, without much success. She saw him glance her way and nod. She nodded back, then tore off her soiled gloves and replaced them with a clean pair.

A male driver in his fifties moaned for help from his badly damaged Volvo. He'd managed to open his door and now he was crying, "Oh, my God. It hurts so bad. I know I'm going to die!"

Eyeing his pallor and noting the way he was clutching his left shoulder with his right hand, Jackie was immediately concerned. "Sir, I'm a nurse. Maybe I can help. Can you tell me what the problem is?"

"The pressure..." he gasped. "I can hardly breathe."

"In your chest?"

He nodded.

"And your arm?"

He nodded again.

"Any history of heart disease, sir?"

"Yeah. I have angina. About five years ago I had a heart attack. It was just like this. Oh, God, I'm going to die this time, I know it."

"Do you have your nitro spray?"

"In the glove compartment. I can't—"

"That's okay. I'll get it." She ran to the other door and quickly found the spray. "Here. Take this."

He eagerly sprayed two shots under his tongue. Almost immediately he showed improvement. As an added precaution, Jackie gave him an aspirin to chew, then she flagged down an uninjured accident victim and asked her to sit with the man until the paramedics arrived. She scribbled quickly on a Post-It note from her kit and handed it to the quiet young woman.

"Give this to the paramedics when they arrive so they'll know what I've done." She patted the man's hand reassuringly, then moved on again.

This time she could hear a woman calling for help. "Get me out of here! Get me out!"

She was in the front seat of a small two-door car and several people were trying to open one of the doors without success. Jackie rushed over.

When they saw her first-aid kit and the stethoscope strung around her neck, the group of people stepped aside to allow Jackie access to the driver's side of the totaled vehicle. The damage to the car was so severe, it seemed impossible the woman inside could still be alive. But she was alive, and conscious, too, though frantic with fear, pain or probably both.

"My legs are trapped. I can't move them!"

The woman was strapped in her seat and her air bag had deployed, saving her from massive head and neck injuries. But Jackie didn't discount the possibility that there could be injury to the spinal cord.

"I know you must be in terrible pain, miss, but we'd better not move you until the paramedics show up. Can you wiggle your toes?" she asked hopefully.

"Nothing! Am I going to be paralyzed?"

She was good-looking, probably in her mid-twenties. "Perhaps you've lost feeling due to a lack of circulation," Jackie said, offering hope. She glanced around at the crowd. "Anyone got any thick jackets, towels or blankets?"

"I have some towels. They're a little damp…" A woman in a sundress, who'd obviously spent the day on the beach, offered two striped towels from a wicker bag.

"That's fine." Jackie took them gratefully and did her best to immobilize the young woman's neck.

The reassuring sounds of sirens were all around them now. But how were the ambulances going to be able to transport these people to the hospital with any speed? The traffic snarl continued on both sides of the highway for as far as she could see. She wondered if her brother Nate was on duty today. Boy, she could sure use his help out here.

Jackie stood, pressing a hand firmly to the side of her neck where the muscles were throbbing now. She'd worked her way right up to the tractor-trailer unit. The driver seemed to be okay. He was upright in the sideways cab, free of his seat belt and talking to two men who'd emerged from their wrecked vehicles to give him a blast.

Over on the far left, she watched as the paramedics spilled from two ambulances. Jackie almost cried with relief when she saw her tall, dark-haired younger brother emerge from the first vehicle, dressed in his navy uniform.

"Nate!"

Somehow, above all the noise and commotion, he heard her. She saw him frown.

"Jackie? What the hell…?"

She wound her way through the maze of demolished cars and accident victims. "I was here when it happened, Nate. My car is probably totaled, but I'm fine."

Her brother engulfed her in a hug and she winced at the pain that shot from her neck down her shoulder. She pulled away gently. "I've been around to most of the serious victims." She told him about the bleeding boy who was in shock, the man who was almost for sure having a heart attack, the trapped young woman who couldn't feel her legs.

"Good work, Jackie." Nate patted her shoulder, already signaling the other paramedics where to go. She left her brother to do his job, thankful that he was here, though still concerned about the inevitable long transport times.

About to make her way back to her car, Jackie paused when she heard a faint wail. Unlike the cries and moans around her, this one was higher pitched and as steady as a stream of water from a faucet. The sound was unmistakable to anyone who'd heard it before.

A baby.

Jackie's heart jammed up in her throat. The cry was coming from the other side of the tipped trailer. Dropping to her knees, she could see the front end of a station wagon that had been trapped under the collapsed rig. She tried calling out to the mother or father of the infant, but no one responded.

Sick fear momentarily froze her as she eyed the huge barrier that stood in her way. She had to get to that baby. But the vehicle was sandwiched between the overturned rig and the burned-out sedan.

Suddenly she felt a hand on her shoulder. She turned and looked up with disbelief. It was the motorcycle cop. He'd removed his helmet and his light brown hair was damp with sweat.

Their eyes met with common understanding. He'd heard the cries, too.

"You a doctor?"

"Nurse."

He paused, then nodded. "Okay, then. Let's help that kid." He laced his fingers and, without a second thought, she placed her sandaled foot on the perch.

"One, two, three…" He heaved as she reached up

and soon she was standing on what had once been the side of the trailer. She scrambled quickly across it, the metal hard on her bare knees. The cop followed. He was right next to her when she finally spotted the remains of the trapped vehicle. The front half was completely crushed under the back end of the trailer. In the rear seat, she could see the outline of an infant carrier.

"Shit."

She shared the cop's opinion.

He held out his hand again and helped her down to solid ground. "Be careful of the glass," he said. He shrugged out of his leather jacket and used it to kneel on so he could take a look inside the front seat of the car.

She turned away, focusing on the wailing baby. The rear door was jammed, but the window had smashed into a million pieces. Heeding the cop's warning, she slipped off a sandal and used it to sweep away the residue. Thanks to safety regulations, vehicles were now manufactured with window glass that disintegrated into relatively harmless pebbles. Still, she was careful to ensure that the glass pellets fell to the ground and not into the car with the baby.

"Hey, sweetie," she called softly. "Are you okay in there?"

The wailing halted, but only for a split second. She was encouraged that the baby had responded, even momentarily, to the sound of her voice. She leaned in through the window for a closer look.

"Oh, God." Instinctively she pulled back. Closed her eyes.

"What's wrong?" Still on the ground trying to see into the front seat, the cop must have heard her cry out.

"This baby's only a few months old. His face is covered with blood." She steeled herself to reach out to the infant. Pulling aside the blue blanket he'd been wrapped in allowed her a closer look at his face. Shattered glass lay all around him, but not from the window. These shards were from something else.

She spotted the plastic frame of a mirror and shook her head at the mother's foolishness.

"You're going to be okay, sweetie. Let me see if I can get you out of that car seat." She would have preferred to leave him in the padded carrier, but no way would she be able to get the awkward thing through the window. Quickly she released the metal catch at the bottom, then pushed aside the canvas straps.

"Okay, baby. You're coming out." As gently as possible, she lifted the light little thing from the seat and through the window.

Finally the wailing stopped as she held the child in her arms. There were more cuts on his arms and legs, and some on his scalp, too. Jackie checked for slivers of glass, wishing for a table, direct lighting and good quality sterilized tweezers.

"He okay?" The cop was standing again. Keeping a careful distance from her and the baby, he shook the glass out of his jacket, then slipped it back on.

Jackie continued her inspection of the infant. "Lots of lacerations, but most of them superficial, I hope. I'm most worried about his eyes."

Both were puffy, but the right one was also bleeding. She mopped up the blood with some gauze and saw that his eyelid was lacerated and, even worse, a fragment of glass appeared lodged in his cornea.

She wrapped the blue blanket around his tiny body, frowning at the way the little guy turned his head from the slightest exposure to sunlight.

Not a good sign. Poor babe.

"If his injuries are as extensive as I fear, he needs to be seen by a surgeon right away." What she could see of the injury was bad enough. But she was more worried about potential damage to the internal ocular structures.

"Poor kid."

She thought the cop was referring to the baby's injuries, but then she noticed his gaze dwelling on the front half of the crushed vehicle.

Oh, no. "The driver?"

He shook his head gravely. "I'm afraid the baby's mother is dead."

CHAPTER THREE

LIFE WAS SO UNFAIR. Jackie knew this. But why, why did the mother of a helpless infant have to die in such a senseless manner?

Jackie's parents had been killed in an accident, too, when she was just a toddler. Her heart went out to the little one in her arms, who wouldn't have even a vague memory of his mother's voice to sustain him in his life.

"His eyes are really getting puffy," the cop observed, folding back a corner of the blanket to get a look at the infant's blood-smeared face.

Was this kid going to end up blind on top of everything else? Not if she could help it. "We've got to get him to the ER. But look at this mess!"

To the far left, a painfully slow procession of emergency vehicles was finally showing up on the scene. But it would be a while before they were able to deliver patients to the hospital.

"I could transport you pretty fast on my bike." He pointed. "It's back about fifty yards."

Jackie didn't hesitate. At this point there were no other reasonable options. "Let's do it."

The cop took the baby, freeing her to scramble back over the rig. On an impulse, she'd grabbed the diaper bag in the car, and now slipped it over her shoulder, then reached out for the baby so the cop could follow. In less than a minute they'd woven their way to his parked bike.

"My helmet won't fit you," he apologized. And of course they had nothing for the baby. "But I'll get you there safe."

Their eyes met, and in those few seconds she reminded herself that though this man was a cop, he was also a stranger. She knew nothing about him except what she'd seen since the accident.

But what she *had* seen inspired trust. He was tall, fit and strong, and so far he'd reacted to every situation they'd encountered with calm intelligence, unselfish bravery.

"Let's do it." Without another word, she slid onto the back of his bike, the baby sandwiched between them. Placing one hand on his firm shoulder, clutching the infant with the other, she took a deep breath. "Okay."

He glanced back once, to make sure she was securely seated, then took off, hugging the shoulder of the road. They passed the sedan that had been burning briskly earlier. Firefighters had managed to haul a hose across the highway and extinguish the flames. Now they were using crowbars to pry off the passenger door.

Jackie turned away. She didn't want an accidental glimpse of whatever charred remains were found in that car. She'd already seen so much pain and suffering, and she knew this was only the beginning. When she made it to the hospital, she would be starting a twelve-hour shift. The people being carried by stretchers into those ambulances would soon be her patients.

Her neck was killing her now. The motorcycle might be a speedy and efficient mode of transportation, but it didn't offer a smooth ride.

Glancing down at the baby tucked against her chest, she saw that the little guy had been lulled to sleep by the movement and noise. *Poor wee thing. Please let him be okay.*

Beneath her left hand, the cop's shoulder felt rigid. Strong. She couldn't resist leaning her head against his back for support. He didn't seem to mind, so she let herself relax against him. It was lucky for her—and this baby—that he'd been on the scene so quickly.

She wondered what his name was, whether he had a family. She guessed he was around her age. She hadn't thought about his looks earlier, but they had registered in some far corner of her mind. Now she recalled light-brown eyes, a high forehead, a mouth that would look fabulous when he smiled.

So far he hadn't had much reason to smile. But she guessed by the faint lines around the corners of his lips that he usually did.

But why was she thinking about him like this? He was probably married. Weren't most people by the time they turned thirty?

She had been married when she was twenty-five.

With lights flashing and sirens blaring, they were attracting quite a lot of attention. People on the sidewalk paused to stare. Cars pulled over to make room and drivers stuck their necks out open windows.

She'd never been so glad to see the pale stucco facade of Courage Bay Hospital. Fortunately the bay driveway to emergency was clear, except for a large white van. As the cop cruised in closer, she noticed the call numbers of a local TV station, KSEA, painted in bold colors on the back of the van. Just then, a camera flash went off in her eyes. She winced and held the baby closer. The cop glided his bike past the reporter, over the sidewalk, right up to the ER doors.

Turning to her, he asked, "You okay?"

She nodded.

"Sorry if that was a little rough."

The journalists were back, this time with video cameras. The cop put up an arm to block her from their view. "Excuse me, ma'am…sir," he said in a polite but firm tone, "but we've got a medical emergency here."

"Is the baby okay?"

"Are you the baby's mother?"

"What's the situation back at the accident scene? Anybody killed?"

From under the cop's protective arm, Jackie did her best to ignore the questions. Inside the ER, she was finally on home turf and knew exactly what to do. She raced to the admittance desk. Stout, grayhaired Izzy was working triage today.

"What's wrong, Jackie?" She eyed the bundle in her arms. "Who is that?"

"I have no idea."

"Oh, my Lord. Here." Izzy passed a clean tissue for Jackie to mop up the fresh blood on the baby's face. "What happened?"

"I was in a car crash on the PCH."

"We heard about that. We're expecting the ambulances shortly. So you got caught in the pileup? How terrible. And the poor baby... Oh, my Lord, he doesn't look older than a couple of months."

Jackie lowered her voice. "His mother died in the crash. I think he may have a glass shard embedded in his right cornea. I haven't had a chance to examine him properly yet."

Izzy gave her another clean tissue. "We'll get a pediatrician right away. How'd you get here so fast?" Izzy's gaze slid over to the police officer.

He nodded and held out his hand. "Officer Guthrie." He turned to Jackie and added, "*Casey* Guthrie."

She had to swallow before she could reply in kind. "I'm Jackie Kellison."

It only took a few seconds to exchange their names, but Jackie had the weird sense of falling into a time vortex where the moment felt long and heavy with importance. Then the baby stirred in her arms.

She faced Izzy again. "Officer Guthrie was the first one on the scene. He gave us a ride on his motorbike."

"Well, that explains the hairdo."

Jackie supposed more hair was out of her ponytail than in. She'd also lost her sunglasses in the fray and her cotton shorts and blouse were smeared with blood. None of that mattered at the moment.

Izzy shoved aside the paperwork she'd been dealing with. "Come on, we'll get that little one into an examining room." She glanced back at the cop still standing by her desk. "Nice to have met you, Officer Guthrie."

The baby started crying again and Jackie hurried after Izzy. She managed one last glance at the motorcycle cop, regretting she'd had no chance to say a proper goodbye. They'd made a good team.

He smiled at her, and his smile *was* nice, just as she'd thought. Too bad she probably wouldn't see him again.

IN THE SMALL examining room, Jackie was finally able to take a good look at her patient. While waiting for the physician, she cleaned the abrasions on the baby's face and hands, ensuring that she hadn't missed any tiny pieces of glass. Tenderly she undressed the fussing infant, inhaling with mild surprise when she unfastened the diaper. Well, the baby was a girl. And her diaper was sodden. When had her mother last changed it?

Jackie cleaned the bright pink bottom gently, noticing an oval-shaped birthmark on one chubby thigh. The child was working herself into a frenzy again. Would the damn doctor never get here?

CASEY LINGERED IN THE ER waiting room for a while. He made a call to the station and confirmed that since he'd been officially off duty for the past hour, he wouldn't be part of the team investigating the collision.

He passed on the information about the burning sedan, how there'd been a second explosion following the first. He'd seen cars catch fire because of a leaking fuel line before, but this one hadn't fit the pattern.

After he'd concluded that call, he made another, leaving a message at the hotel where his friends were staying. "Sorry, something came up at work. A collision on PCH. I won't be able to join you guys tonight."

There was really no reason for him to cancel. He still had time to get home and shower and go out tonight. But he didn't want to leave the hospital.

He wanted to make sure the baby was okay. Yeah, that was part of it, but he didn't try to kid himself that that was the whole reason.

Truth was, he wanted to see that nurse again. Jackie Kellison. Hell, she sure was something. She'd been unstoppable at the accident scene. He was willing to bet she'd saved more than one life today with her quick thinking and fast action.

Never mind that she'd been a victim in the accident herself. Beyond the emotional distress of the experience, she'd obviously suffered whiplash. He'd noticed her holding her head tighter and tighter as time went on. That ride on his bike must have been murder.

He'd liked the way she'd rested her head on his

back, though. He had a feeling Jackie didn't lean on many people and he was glad he'd been one of them.

Anyway, she'd been in the accident and helped all those people at the scene, and now it appeared she was prepared to put in her full shift. Which only made him admire her more.

The desperate crescendo of sirens told him the accident victims were finally about to arrive. Tired after his long day, yet unable to relax, Casey began pacing. He wished there was something he could do to help. Waiting wasn't his strong suit.

Perhaps he ought to go home and have that shower, and maybe a good long nap, too. But he couldn't take the chance of missing Jackie, so he bought himself a coffee from the vending machine, then found he couldn't drink it.

He tossed out the paper cup, wondering why he didn't just go on his way. Izzy was shooting him quizzical glances, as if she, too, couldn't figure out why he was still hanging around. She'd come over earlier to tell him the baby was about to go into the operating room. Later, she'd be transferred to the hospital's infant care wing.

She. Despite the blue blanket, the baby was a girl. Shouldn't have made any difference, but somehow he'd felt even more protective once he'd heard that. He hoped the doctor operating on her was good, that he was well rested and at the top of his game.

An hour went by, maybe two. Finally his patience was rewarded when Jackie came out to grab a can of cola from a vending machine in the hall. Dressed in scrubs, she leaned against the machine with exhaustion, a hand on her neck as she waited for the can to drop.

"Sore, huh?"

Her head shot up at his unexpected presence and she winced.

"Sorry. Shouldn't have snuck up on you." He wanted to make her sit down for a minute. Maybe get some ice for that neck. Or massage it for her. Instead he leaned over to snag her cola out of the machine. When he handed it to her, she pressed the cool can against the side of her neck.

"You should be at home, looking after yourself."

"I'm fine," she insisted. "It's just a pulled muscle. I consider myself lucky."

Whiplash would send most accident victims running for the nearest liability lawyer. Casey's admiration for the woman increased. "How's it going in there?"

"Not too bad. The burn victim…" She squeezed her eyes shut as if blocking a horrible mental picture. "He and our baby's mom are the only fatalities. The really good news is that we had a young woman trapped in a car who couldn't move her legs, but it turns out her injuries won't be permanent."

"What about the rig driver?"

"Amazingly, he walked away with minor cuts and a few bruises."

"Life makes no sense sometimes."

She looked at him as if what he had said was somehow profound. "Yes. Like that poor mother. Now that she's dead, who's going to look after her baby?"

He encountered tragedies like this all the time in his work. She must, too. Yet he had to agree that this particular situation hit harder than most.

"With any luck she has a good father," he said.

"I hope they find him soon. Though I sure wouldn't want to be the one to tell him what happened."

He nodded, feeling again the sense of affinity that they'd shared at the accident scene. They'd been strangers, tossed into circumstances beyond their control, but their impulses had been identical. To help as many people as they could.

And now that the emergency was over, Casey was left with the strong feeling that he needed to see this woman again. Not because she was pretty, or sexy, though she was both those things. No, he felt a pull that had nothing to do with the usual reasons he sought out a woman.

"Jackie, I—"

She shifted her gaze from him to the floor and backed up a step. The movements were slight, but enough to make his confidence falter.

"I've got to get back in there. We need to treat a couple of fractured bones. Our baby's still in the operating room…"

Our baby. He liked that she'd said it that way, connecting the two of them to the child they'd saved. "Is she okay? Do you think I could see her?"

The expression in her eyes softened. "That's nice of you to be concerned. But her operation won't be over for a while yet. I'm not sure if they'll allow visitors after that."

"Well, until they locate her next of kin, I feel kind of responsible for the squirt."

"I do, too. But they will find her father soon, don't you think?"

"Probably working on it right now."

Jackie started to leave, then turned back. "Thanks for getting us to the hospital so quickly."

Seeing Jackie smile at him, Casey felt an unaccustomed twisting of his heart. He really did feel the most inexplicable concern for that child—a paternal response that was shockingly out of character. He hadn't been faking it just to win Jackie over.

But he had to admit that in the past, he wouldn't have been above using tactics like that.

He suddenly felt ashamed.

"Jackie?"

She paused again, and he could tell she was impatient to move on.

"What time does your shift end?"

"Not for ten more hours. It was nice to meet you, Officer Guthrie."

Then she was gone, having made it all too clear that she had no intention of seeing him again.

CASEY RODE ACROSS the street to the gas station, where he washed his regulation bike and filled it with gas. He chatted briefly with the woman at the till—he and Debbie were big fans of the Mighty Ducks—then headed the few blocks back to the station to park his bike in the garage and hand in his tickets for the day.

He found his lieutenant reading copy straight from the fax machine. Tank Gordon, in his forties but so clean-cut he could pass for ten years younger, checked him out.

"That was quite a mess on PCH today. You okay? What happened?"

"I'm fine. I was on my way back to the station at the end of my shift. The collision happened right in front of my eyes. First a sedan burst into flames. A tractor-trailer rig right next to it lost control and overturned. Cars piled up on both sides of the highway." He shook his head, remembering.

"You left the scene without clearing an exit route for the emergency vehicles."

Casey frowned. Was he being reprimanded here? "Backup had arrived, sir. We had lots of men on hand. I figured it was more important to get an injured baby to the hospital."

"I heard." The lieutenant was holding a grin in check.

"Huh?"

"They're running footage on the evening news. Picked yourself a pretty little nurse, I'll say that for you. Reminds me of Sally Fields in her younger days."

Used to being teased about his ability to attract lovely women, Casey bristled this time. "Jackie Kellison was amazing out there. I'll bet she saved more than a couple of lives."

"So you didn't notice her huge brown eyes? Or long, bare legs?"

"Cut the B.S., Lieutenant. In case you've forgotten, we had an injured baby on that bike, too. Her mother was killed in the crash."

The lieutenant sobered with that. "Yeah. I know."

"Any luck locating next of kin?" In those hours he'd paced the ER floor, Casey had worried a lot about the father. He couldn't stop imagining the man coming home from work and wondering where his wife and baby were. Then the phone would ring and his life, as he'd known it, would come to an end....

Lieutenant Gordon turned to watch the fax machine slowly regurgitate a new sheet of paper. "Actually, the baby's family is turning out to be a problem."

"What do you mean, *a problem?*"

"We haven't been able to ID the woman. And that car she was driving?" Gordon pulled out the latest fax and handed it to him. "Take a look at this."

JACKIE'S SHIFT ENDED at dawn. She didn't change out of her uniform since the shorts and top she'd been wearing yesterday afternoon were too torn and bloody to salvage. At the water fountain, she stopped to pop two muscle relaxants. She'd considered taking them earlier in her shift, but had worried that the medication might make her drowsy.

As a result she could barely move her head more than a couple of inches to either side. She hadn't been this bad at the beginning of her shift, but now her muscles were seizing in protest. Driving would be impossible, but that was okay.

She no longer owned a car.

Declining a sympathetic colleague's offer of a ride home, she took the stairs up to the infant care ward on the third floor. She had to see the baby to find out about his—no, *her*—eyes.

She checked the board at the nursing station and saw an infant listed as "Jane Doe." She nodded to a nurse sitting behind a computer monitor. The buxom woman, in her early forties, was ponderously inputting chart information into the system.

"Excuse me. Is Jane Doe the baby from the accident on PCH yesterday?" Twelve hours had passed since Jackie's shift had begun. The accident had occurred on Monday, so it was now Tuesday morning, very early.

The nurse stopped typing. She seemed glad for the interruption and eyed Jackie curiously. "Yes, poor thing, that's her. The cops still haven't figured out who she is."

"But the accident happened over twelve hours ago." Something was wrong here. "The mother died in the crash, but surely they must have located her father by now." Her father and, Jackie hoped, a mess of brothers and sisters, aunts and uncles. As far as she was concerned, the more family the better.

"Well, the cop who keeps checking up on her is doing a good job looking after her for the time being."

Cop? Was Casey Guthrie…? She shot a speculative glance down the corridor.

"He's in with her right now," the nurse confirmed. "Why don't you go say hi? You two looked real good together on the six o'clock news."

CHAPTER FOUR

JACKIE REGISTERED the woman's teasing words with some confusion—until she remembered the reporters who'd been waiting outside the ER when Casey had driven up to the door yesterday.

It felt like forever ago now.

So they'd made the regional news broadcast. That meant her older brother Kell would know what had happened and be worrying. Of course, Nate had probably told him by now anyway. She'd have to phone them both.

"Thanks." A hand to her sore neck, she set off down the wide corridor. The name Jane Doe was posted on the wall next to the second room on the left. She tapped the partially open door, then stepped inside.

And held her breath.

A tall, athletic man in jeans and a white T-shirt was holding a blanket-wrapped bundle and rocking back and forth on his heels like a seasoned parent. He held a cold compress gently against the patch on the baby's eye. Jackie thought he might have been humming a soft tune, but he stopped as soon as he noticed her.

"Hi," she said.

Casey Guthrie had changed out of uniform and cleaned himself up. Oh, did he look good. Now Jackie did care about her ratty hair and her awful, soiled uniform. She pulled out the elastic from her ponytail and tried to run her fingers through her hair. She couldn't.

"Hi," he said softly.

"How's our Janey?" Jackie moved close enough to brush her fingers over the fuzz on the baby's head. Though she'd expected the baby to wear an eye patch, the sight of it made her own eyes tear. She distracted herself by referring to the baby's chart.

She checked the list of medications and saw everything she would have expected from mydriatics and cycloplegics, which would keep the pupil dilated, to the antibiotics that would ward off infection.

"She'll have to wear that pressure patch for at least a day," Jackie said.

"Yes. I was here when the surgeon stopped by to see how she was doing. As you suspected, there was a glass shard in her eye." Casey broke the news in a quiet, sympathetic tone. "The doctors are hoping damage won't be permanent, but at this point they just don't know."

"Oh, Casey." She moved in close enough to kiss the little one's forehead. "Does she seem to be in pain?"

"Mostly she's been sleeping. Nurses have been in here 'round the clock. One just left to get a clean dressing."

Jackie noticed Casey start his rocking motion again. "You're good with kids. Do you have any?"

Though he didn't wear a ring, she wasn't going to simply assume he wasn't married.

He grinned. "No wife. No kids. But I'm glad to get a little practice in. It may come in handy when my big brother starts a family."

She noticed he didn't say when *he* had kids. Did that mean he wasn't planning a family for himself? A nurse bustled into the room then, and he handed Janey over to her—not before touching his forefinger to the side of the baby's cheek.

Again, Jackie felt thick, bittersweet emotion stealing over her. Where was this child's father? She blinked away a threatening tear, then noticed Casey wasn't gazing at the baby anymore but at her.

Oh, Lord. He must be appalled at how awful she looked.

"I haven't had a minute to myself since I saw you last," she confessed. "I know I look like hell." The accident had strained the ER department to the limit, even though they'd called in extra nurses and doctors.

"You were incredible."

Casey's eyes shone with admiration and, oddly, that made her want to cry again, too. What a crazy day.

"Hardly." She turned to the chart once more, not knowing what else to do, and stared at the blurred lines of writing.

"You were a real hero today."

"No." She wasn't. She'd helped some people a little, but there'd been too many she couldn't help. That poor man incinerated in his own car. And Janey's mother crushed and trapped under the tractor-trailer rig...

She blinked rapidly, but still felt her eyes growing damp.

No, she wasn't a hero. She'd only done her job, and now she felt so...so tired. And more taxed emotionally than she'd admitted to her co-workers.

"Let me take you home." Casey put an arm over her shoulders and pulled her close. She was reminded of riding with him on the bike, leaning against his back for support. Strange that she'd felt comfortable enough to do that. She barely knew Casey Guthrie.

Gently she eased out from under his arm. "It's nice of you to offer. But I can take a cab." It was more than nice of him to offer, actually. If he'd been at the hospital for most of the night, he had to be exhausted, too.

She attempted a smile and a feeble joke. "Anyway, I don't think I can take another ride on your motorbike."

He laughed. "That belongs to the department. I do own a bike of my own, a sweet little Harley that I know you'd love." He winked, acknowledging the joke. "But I brought my car this time. Come on."

There was no polite way to avoid walking down the corridor with him and taking the elevator together to street level. Outside, in the faint light of dawn, he led her to the visitors' lot and she made out the sleek lines of a luxury sports car.

A white convertible Saab. She thought sadly of her totaled Mazda. "Nice car. I didn't know cops were paid that well."

"We aren't." He unlocked the doors and held the passenger one open for her. She hesitated, then decided she had no energy to argue the point. If he wanted to be chivalrous, then she would let him. He waited until she was settled, then closed the door gently and loped to the driver's side.

"As a man with no ties or responsibilities, which is the way my big brother, Adam, always describes me, I can afford to spend most of my money on toys."

Toys meaning fast cars and motorcycles. And women, too? Jackie could only speculate. Now that the emergency was over, she was able to fully appreciate just what a hunk this motorcycle cop was. Besides his great build and hot smile, his eyes held a certain sparkle that she guessed would appeal to women. No doubt he had a very active social life.

Unlike her.

She gave him directions to her condo, a few blocks back from the beach. She'd moved here two years ago, after selling the house she'd lived in with Andrew. At the time, leaving had been painful, but no way could she have stayed. Even packing had been more than she could endure. Her brothers, bless their hearts, had taken care of all of that, including the garage, Andrew's study, his clothes…

Don't go there, Jackie.

As she concentrated on relaxing her muscles, she

realized that the pain in her neck was easing. The medication she'd taken must have finally kicked in. She leaned back against the leather seat and closed her eyes. Casey, thank goodness, took the corners slow and easy. She wondered if he would drop her off on the street or come up to her door.

From what she'd seen of his manners so far, he would insist on walking her to the door. At which time she would thank him politely and he would leave. She would grab a quick bite to eat, then crash into bed.

Only, what if he asked if she would see him again?

He won't. I'm not his type.

She was sure she'd pegged him right as a real ladies' man. And she didn't date that sort. Never had. Not even the bold and daring old Jackie had ever cared for that kind of a guy.

Okay, if that's true, then stop thinking about him. And definitely stop looking at him as if you'd like to eat him for breakfast.

She tried thinking about what she *would* eat when she was home. What, if anything, did she have in her fridge right now? Her intended trip to the grocery store yesterday had been curtailed when the unseasonably warm weather had drawn her to the beach instead.

"Hungry?" Casey asked.

"You must have been reading my mind. I was trying to remember what I had in my fridge."

"And?"

"Condiments, mostly," she admitted. "Though I may have a pizza in the freezer."

Just saying the word *pizza* made her realize how famished she was. Several hours ago she'd grabbed an energy bar and supplemented it with two or three colas since. But that was all.

"That sounds good," Casey said.

A frozen pizza? Was he serious? "Have you had breakfast?"

"No breakfast. Or dinner, either, come to think of it. What with running back and forth between the station and the hospital—with one quick trip home to change—I don't think I've eaten in over twelve hours."

No wonder the frozen pizza sounded good to him. "Well, in that case—"

"Thought you'd never ask. I'd love to join you."

His grin was cheeky and sexy at the same time. She wondered if there was a woman alive who could avoid a man like this. And more important, why would she want to?

Casey was unattached, he was gorgeous, he had a good job. There was no reason in the world she shouldn't take the opportunity to get to know him better.

No reason, that is, except for the buzzing of nervous fear in her stomach. It was past time for her to start dating again—everyone said so.

But she needed to ease into the dating scene with caution. Maybe start with a nice, quiet accountant. Work her way up to a dentist. Then, maybe…maybe, she'd be ready to date a cop. One who rode motorcycles no less.

Though, maybe she was jumping the gun here. What made her think this was a date? She and Casey had shared a harrowing experience. As a result, he'd offered her a ride home. Now he wanted to join her for pizza because he really was starving, just as she was.

As her condo complex came into view, she directed him to the visitor parking lot under the building. They rode the elevator to the second floor, then walked the long hall to her corner unit.

"It's small," she said as she unlocked the front door. "But I do have an ocean view from the bedroom."

"Hmm. I'd like to see that."

Her hand froze. She lifted her head. He was smiling at her, that sparkly expression in his eyes again, as if he thought she was something special.

At the hospital when he'd looked at her that way, she'd assumed he was admiring her medical expertise. Now she had to wonder.

"Be careful, Officer Guthrie. I'm going to think you're flirting with me."

He laughed. "Finally she gets it."

Oh. Her heart skipped with an excitement she hadn't felt in years and years. *Okay, so maybe he is interested.* She opened the door, suddenly lighthearted. A quick glance at her reflection in the hall mirror brought her down to earth quickly. Oh, Lord, she looked worse than she'd thought. She dropped her keys in the wicker basket by the door and flung her purse on top.

She heard Casey lock the dead bolt behind her and felt a momentary doubt. What did she really know about this man?

She shook off the fear. He was a cop for heaven's sake. How dangerous could he be?

CASEY LIKED JACKIE'S HOME. It was casual and comfortable, without much in the way of decorating froufrou. Her slip-covered couch looked inviting, the wooden table next to it seemed like something a person could put his feet up on without scratching or breaking anything. He strode to the window, but from this angle could only see the apartment building across the street.

As Jackie headed for the counter dividing living room from kitchen, she paused by the flashing red light on her phone. That light made him wonder. Jackie didn't wear any rings, but maybe she took them off for work. Or maybe she had a boyfriend who hadn't yet figured out what a treasure she was and staked his claim.

"This is probably a call from my older brother. Excuse me a minute while I let him know I'm okay."

Pretending a casual interest in the volumes on her bookshelves, he unabashedly listened as she picked up the receiver and made the connection.

"Kell, it's me, Jackie. Sorry I missed your call. My shift just ended and I wanted to let you and Nate know that I'm okay. My car, though…" She sighed. "I'm afraid it's totaled. I'll have to buy a new one."

She kept the conversation brief, not mentioning

the fact that she had a visitor. After she'd hung up, she went to the stove and turned on the oven. "I'm going to shower and change, really quick. Would you pop the pizza in when the oven's ready? Help yourself to something to drink. I have orange juice and cola and I keep filtered water in the fridge."

"Thanks." He watched her disappear down the hall and soon heard the pounding of water from the shower in the bathroom.

He thought about her conversation with her brother. She'd been upset about her car. Casey wondered if it was too soon in their relationship to offer to help her shop for a new vehicle. He had some contacts at a few of the dealerships. As soon as he had the thought, he laughed at himself.

His usual reaction when he met a pretty new woman was to calculate how much fun he could have without getting in too deep. But he could tell already, Jackie was not going to be just another pretty new woman to him.

Considering he knew that, logic dictated he get out of here while the getting was good. The one problem with that very rational plan was that he didn't want to go. He didn't want to be anywhere except here, with her. Besides, he still hadn't told her the latest development in locating Janey's family.

He strolled to the kitchen, noticing little things like the vibrant lime-green of her tea towels and an opened envelope on the counter by her phone. The return address was from a Dr. Michael Temple, clinical psychiatrist. It looked like the sort of envelope that would contain an invoice for services rendered.

Ignoring the urge to check to see if his hunch was right, he pulled the boxed pizza from the freezer and removed the wrappings. Once he had their meal in the oven, he returned to the task of inspecting her bookshelf. He wanted clues about this woman. Her novels were mostly bestsellers, like the kinds he enjoyed. Lots of action, mystery, suspense.

Interesting, but he needed more personal information. He picked up a framed photograph of Jackie and two men, obviously her brothers. Both were good-looking guys, with thick dark hair like their sister. He was surprised when he recognized the older one from the police station. Robert Kellison—Kell—rode mounted patrol. Jackie's other brother looked familiar, too, but Casey couldn't place where he'd seen him before.

The photograph had been taken in the country, probably at a ranch, since the three were posed on and around a wooden fence. There was a horse in the background, a real beauty.

They looked like a close-knit bunch, he thought, noticing the easy way Jackie's hand rested on Kell's shoulder and the protective way both men leaned in toward their sister. He set the photo down, then was about to turn on the television to pass the time when he caught a glimpse of something silver behind a crystal vase filled with colored glass disks. Was that another picture frame? He was reaching to move the vase when Jackie came out dressed in gray sweatpants that hugged her hips and a short white T-shirt that didn't quite meet her navel. With her damp hair brushed back behind her ears, her thickly lashed eyes appeared huge.

"Something smells good."

He'd forgotten about the pizza. He dashed back to the kitchen and pulled it from the oven, thankful that only the edges of the crust had begun to darken. She took plates from a cupboard and put cutlery on the counter, but neither of them bothered with anything but a napkin. She inhaled her first slice standing next to him. By the second, they were on the floor in the living room. She couldn't finish the third, but he did. And a fourth, too.

"You *were* hungry," she teased.

"Apparently so."

Her long legs were spread out on the carpet as she leaned her back against the sofa. He noticed she was still careful about how she moved her head. After cleaning his hands on an extra napkin, he went to sit on the sofa behind her.

"Tell me how this feels." Slipping his fingers under the neckline of her T-shirt, he massaged the muscles of her shoulders. He could feel the clenched knot to the right of her neck. Gently he worked his thumbs in opposing circles. It took several minutes before she finally relaxed.

"That feels great."

"Good." He kept his touch gentle, enjoying the soft feel of her skin, the minty scent of her shampoo, the warmth of her body between his legs.

"What a crazy day."

She sounded drowsy. Really, he should leave and

let her get some sleep. But he lingered for ten more minutes…fifteen. Finally she leaned forward, out of his grasp.

"That was so nice, Casey. But we should probably…"

She got to her feet awkwardly, leaving him no choice but to stand, as well.

"Sorry," he said. "I've stayed too long."

"No. It's been nice."

Her smile was tentative, but the moment they made eye contact, he felt again the novel certainty that this woman was somehow different from every other woman he'd met.

"Do you feel it, too?" he asked.

"What?"

He should have dropped it then, but something inside him wouldn't let him. "That it wasn't just a coincidence we were both on the scene of that collision today."

"You think we were meant to help those people?"

"Yes." And also that they were meant to meet each other. But he could tell from the way she'd begun to back away from him again that it was too soon for him to say something nearly that serious.

"Well, I'm not sure that it was fate or anything. But I'm glad we were able to be of some use." She folded the pizza box and stuffed it into the garbage.

"Are you going to visit the baby again?" he asked.

"Yes. Definitely. I wonder if they've found her family yet. Do you know why it's taking so long?"

"Her mother didn't have any ID on her," he explained. "Not a purse, not a wallet, not even a driver's license in her pocket."

She frowned. "That's strange."

"Tell me about it."

"Were there any registration papers in the glove compartment?"

"Yeah. According to them, the car belongs to a Myra Bedford in Los Angeles."

"But you don't think the woman driving the car was Myra?"

"We know she wasn't. About an hour after the accident, Myra Bedford reported her vehicle stolen."

Now Jackie was really looking confused. He didn't blame her. The situation was bizarre to say the least.

"Myra Bedford was visiting her daughter in Courage Bay. She went shopping in the Super Value Mall with her three-month-old grandson yesterday afternoon, and when she came out of the mall, she found her Taurus wagon missing."

"The baby's mother stole it?" Jackie sounded skeptical.

"That's the way it looks."

"But why would she do that?"

"I'm guessing because there was an infant car seat in the back that she could use for Janey."

Jackie shook her head. "That's why she picked the Taurus. But why steal a car in the first place?"

"People steal cars for a variety of reasons. Some just want a joyride."

"Surely not in this case."

"Well, another common reason to steal a car is because you're about to commit a crime."

"You think she was on her way to rob a bank or something? With a two-month-old in the back seat? Casey, who *was* this woman?"

"That's exactly what we're trying to figure out. Only so far, we really don't have a clue."

CHAPTER FIVE

JACKIE DIDN'T HAVE MANY resources left. The day had been long and demanding both physically and emotionally. But now, faced with these new and puzzling facts, her mind felt sharp and clear.

"I can't understand why a mother of a sweet little girl would steal a car."

"We don't know the circumstances. Maybe she was pushed into the crime. Maybe she was desperate."

Jackie paced the narrow hall between kitchen and living room. The situation, she realized, could be even worse. "What if Janey's father is abusive? Maybe her mother was running away from him. And now that she's dead, there will be no one to protect the baby..."

"Stop, Jackie. Please." Casey put his hands on her shoulders. "You're exhausted and you're letting your imagination run wild."

"I guess I'm past the point of thinking straight. But that child has suffered so much already—"

"At least we know she's safe for now."

"In the hospital. Yes, that's true."

Casey nodded. "After we get some sleep, we'll check on her again. And I'll phone the station. It shouldn't be much longer before the rest of her family is located. Maybe then we'll find out what gives with the stolen car."

Jackie was now calm, but Casey's hands remained on her shoulders. She felt a little nervous about that, but a strange sort of excitement was involved, too. It was a sensation she hadn't experienced for a long time. After Andrew, she'd been kind of…numb.

"Casey, I—" Experience had taught her it was dangerous to look him straight in the eyes. Now she felt it again, a perilous tingle that she recognized as a pure adrenaline rush.

Was it the sexy cop? The possibility of an engrossing mystery? Or both?

"Whatever happens tomorrow, I'd like to see you again, Jackie."

Casey left no room for her to doubt his intentions this time. His gaze was warm, personal and very interested.

For a long time Jackie had been struggling to make it through each day. Yesterday, with her new car and the beautiful weather, she'd almost felt like her old self again. And now she had this gorgeous man in her living room, asking to see her tomorrow.

Added to everything else—the accident, the problem with Janey, her long shift in the ER—it was just too much.

"I can't—" She stopped, knowing that whatever she said would be the wrong thing. "Let's focus on

Janey for now," she finally told him. "For the time being, we're all she's got."

But then she remembered something important.

"The diaper bag. I wonder if Janey's mother had her ID in there?"

Casey straightened. "Damn. I forgot all about that. Do you still have it?"

"In my locker at work." She clasped a hand to her forehead. "How could I have forgotten?"

"Did you look inside at all?"

"In the examining room I changed Janey's diaper. But there were some compartments I didn't even touch."

"Wouldn't it be great if the mother's wallet was in one of them?"

"Maybe she found carrying a purse as well as a diaper bag too cumbersome."

Their eyes connected and she could tell he was thinking the same thing she was. Sleep. She needed sleep. But the idea of some man pacing the floor of his house, wondering what had happened to his wife and child, was intolerable. She grabbed her keys and the purse she'd so recently put away.

"Ready?" she asked Casey.

"You're something else, Jackie Kellison. Let's go."

THE DIAPER BAG, faded denim with cream-colored plastic lining, was in her locker where she'd left it. Casey stood at Jackie's shoulder as she unzipped each compartment.

In the largest one she found several plush sleepers in assorted pastel colors and two folded flannel blankets. The next compartment held diapers and wet wipes; the next, two clean bottles and some tins of infant formula.

Finally only one small unzipped flap was left to check. Jackie glanced at Casey, swallowed, then inserted her hand into the opening.

No wallet, but there was something. She pulled out a sloppily folded map of Courage Bay. One small section had been circled in red—the exclusive neighborhood of Jacaranda Heights, where multimillion dollar houses sat on bluffs facing out to magnificent ocean views.

"Look at this—" Casey pointed to an address scribbled on the margin of the map "—159 Vista Drive. It's in the circled area."

"Janey's mother was driving north on the freeway when the accident happened." Jackie traced the route with her forefinger. "She could have been heading for the Jacaranda Heights area."

"So maybe the people at one fifty-nine will be able to identify her." As Casey spread open the map to find the original folds, a newspaper clipping fluttered to the floor. Jackie retrieved it.

She frowned, puzzled. "Looks like a photograph from the *Sentinel.*" One of the faces was immediately familiar to her. "This was taken at this year's hospital fund-raiser. That's Callie Baker, chief of staff."

She pointed out the tall slender woman who was offering her cheek to an older man dressed in a tux.

Casey frowned and squinted at the crumpled clipping. "Isn't that our ex-mayor, Wallace Voltz? I met him once at the courthouse when I was a kid. My dad was on city council."

"Yes, you're right. The caption says, 'Callie Baker, chief of staff at Courage Bay Hospital, gracefully accepts a million-dollar donation from Wallace and Abigail Voltz.'"

Casey peered at the picture. "Well, Mr. Voltz looks a lot happier about that than his wife."

Abigail Voltz, the third person in the photo, observed the kiss between her husband and the much younger woman with a resigned expression. Thin and delicate-looking, she had a plain face that even in her youth probably hadn't been pretty.

"You're right. She does seem a little miffed."

"She's the one with all the money, as I recall. Her family was in real-estate development. There was some talk when Wallace Voltz ran his election campaign that he couldn't have won without his wife's financial support."

"I wonder why the baby's mother had this picture with her?"

Casey glanced again at the address. "This is a long shot, but maybe the Voltzes live at 159 Vista Drive? Could she have been on her way to see them?"

"Why would a woman steal a car, then drive her baby to the home of one of Courage Bay's most prestigious residents?"

"Possibly she intended to apply for a job of some

sort. Maybe she was late for the interview and desperate, so she stole the Taurus."

"Let's go talk to Wallace Voltz and find out." Jackie felt excited by the possibility they might be able to track down the identity of the mystery woman.

Casey smiled at her eagerness. "Wouldn't you rather get some sleep? I can drop this off at the station and they'll send someone down to talk to them."

Logically, Jackie knew Casey's plan was the best. But she felt reluctant to let this go. "Do I look tired? I'm not tired. I think we should check it out first. Why waste police time if the map and the address turn out to mean nothing at all?"

"Jackie…"

She could tell he was going to try to talk her out of it. "Aren't you the least bit curious? Come on, Casey."

He smiled and she could tell he was relenting. "My lieutenant is already ticked off about that unorthodox motorcycle ride… You're a bad influence on me, Jackie Kellison."

It had been a long time since she'd been a bad influence on anyone. She liked the feeling. "We'll be saving the police department time and resources. How can that be a bad thing?"

"Chances are this is going to be a dead end anyway. So, what the heck? Okay, Jackie, you win. I'll drive, you navigate." He handed her the map and the newspaper clipping, then shouldered the diaper bag himself.

As they left the hospital, she was secretly amused by the image of the ultra-masculine cop toting a diaper bag. It made for an incongruous picture in some ways, yet was rather endearing, as well.

Seeing Casey's white convertible gleaming in the full morning sun brought on a yearning for her own destroyed car. "That Mazda was the first truly frivolous expenditure I ever made," she sighed.

She couldn't explain to Casey what that car had really meant to her. After years of unhappiness, of blaming herself, she'd finally decided to do her best to let go of the past.

Now, two weeks after taking ownership of her beautiful red convertible, it had been totaled. What message should she take from that? she wondered.

Casey unlocked the door for her, displaying the perfect courtesy she'd noted earlier as he waited for her to be seated before strolling to his side. In one graceful motion he swung himself over the door and into his seat.

"You looked good in that car," Casey said. "We'll have to get you another one."

She noticed his use of the word "we" and shot him a puzzled glance. His returning smile was full of confidence.

"You're not going to be able to get rid of me very easily," he said. "You've realized this by now, I hope."

"You sound pretty sure of yourself."

"Let's put it this way. Last night I started my four days off. I intend to spend as much of that time as possible with you."

Jackie's heart flipped. She had four days off before her next shift, too. Could this be coincidence? Or was the same fate that had landed them in the accident together doing her mischievous work again?

No, no, no. Fate hadn't brought her and Casey together. Even a woman who hadn't dated in about six years, like her, could tell that Casey wasn't the kind of guy fate delivered to your doorstep.

No, Casey was the love-them-and-leave-them sort of man that fate warned you to stay away from. He was most definitely *not* her destiny.

"Let's find Janey's family first," she said finally, "before we worry about anything else."

CASEY WENT OUT of his way to take a route to Jacaranda Heights that did not require them to drive past the scene of yesterday's accident. Jackie thought that was very sweet of him.

He was driving at a leisurely pace, but still the wind was doing a number on her hair. Deciding she didn't want to show up at the Voltz house looking completely disheveled, she opened her purse to search for a scrunchy and quickly fastened her hair into a makeshift ponytail.

Noticing her cell phone, she remembered that she'd spoken to Kell earlier, but hadn't yet called Nate.

"I should check in with my younger brother," she apologized to Casey, pointing at her phone. "He worries even more than Kell."

"Sounds like you have very protective brothers."

For good reason, she thought. Because of the circumstances of their childhood, she, Kell and Nate were closer than most siblings. Since Andrew's death, her brothers had watched over her with the vigilance of a European grandmother. Sometimes it was too much, but mostly she was glad she had family who cared about her.

She hit Nate's number on her speed dial and caught him in the kitchen. She could hear pans banging in the background. Nate was an excellent cook. Actually, Nate was excellent at pretty much everything he did.

"Sorry I didn't get a chance to talk to you again the other day. Just wanted you to know that I was okay. Not my car, though." She sighed about that again, then reminded herself that she should really be thankful. The car, after all, was only metal and glass and it *could* be replaced.

"Yeah, Kell called a while ago and said he'd heard from you. You did good work at the scene, sis. Made my job a lot easier."

They shared impressions about the various accident victims, then Nate switched to something more personal.

"I hear Casey Guthrie gave you and the baby a lift to the hospital."

"You know Casey?"

"Kell does. At least to see him."

Kell worked on mounted patrol out of the same police station, so Jackie had been expecting to get the lowdown eventually.

"Casey Guthrie has earned himself quite a reputation on the force and even among us paramedics."

"For what, Nate?" Bravery? Courage? Fast action in an emergency?

"Well, he's a good cop in a crunch, and his colleagues like him, but he's also a renegade."

Jackie glanced at her companion. "I'm not surprised to hear that."

"Even his own brother, who happens to be chief of detectives, has given up on Casey. The guy doesn't take anything seriously. And I'm not only talking about work. He never comes to any of the department parties without a woman in tow. And, Jackie? It's always a different woman."

Jackie told herself she wasn't disappointed. She'd pretty much figured this out for herself.

"Don't worry. I'm not a child."

"We just don't want to see you hurt. I know we've been encouraging you to start dating again, but not with a guy like this. Ask yourself one question. Is Casey Guthrie someone you can picture in your future?"

"Really, Nate. It's a little early in the game for that, don't you think?"

"Hardly. You're with him right now, aren't you?"

Years of experience told her there was no point in arguing with her perceptive brother. "How could you tell?"

"Your responses to my questions have been a little guarded. Why are you with him, Jackie? Shouldn't you be getting some rest? Unless..."

She could tell he was wondering if she and Casey

were "resting" together. "Nate! How could you even think that? I promise, everything is under control." Jackie closed her tired eyes. She'd been a fool to make this call now. "Nate?"

"Yeah?"

"I'm okay. Really. But I have to go now. I'll call you back tomorrow." She turned off the phone and returned it to her purse.

Casey shot her a questioning glance. "Let me guess. The brothers don't approve?"

She hesitated a moment, then realized there was no point in pretending. "Not hardly."

THE CHIME OF THE DOORBELL startled the entire family. Wallace Voltz put down his Scotch and soda. His wife, Abigail, stared at him with red-rimmed eyes. On the other side of the room, seated at opposite ends of a long leather sofa, his son Bill and daughter-in-law, Sherri-Ann, exchanged heavy, portentous looks.

What were those two up to? They'd been avoiding each other since they'd arrived last night. In a situation like this, you'd think they'd be clinging to one another for support.

Was his son's marriage on the rocks? Wallace didn't understand what had drawn his son to Sherri-Ann in the first place. She was pretty enough, with fine features and auburn hair. But she didn't have the sweet personality of his own Abigail—or the substantial investment accounts, either.

Still, Bill had married her and now they had a child. If he thought it would help, Wallace would have lectured his son about the lifelong responsibilities of family. But he knew Bill wouldn't listen to him.

When his son had turned thirteen, his thought processes had been a mystery to his father. Now, as Bill approached his thirties, he was as much an enigma to Wallace as he'd been as a teenager.

It was different with Abigail. Bill and his mother had always been close. Perhaps he could ask Abigail to talk to their son.

Wallace went to the window and peered through the sheer fabric. "I don't know these people. Maybe we should ignore them."

"We can't," Abigail said sharply. "What if they're..."

She didn't finish her sentence. She didn't need to. Wallace glanced down at his empty hands, wishing he still had the Scotch. It was damn early to be drinking, but under these circumstances, how could he not?

"You're right," he said, trying to project a calm front for his family. "I'll get the door."

He made his way to the foyer, hoping the couple outside were salespeople or some other innocuous visitors. But he didn't think so. They were going to have news; he felt it in his bones.

Please, God, let her be okay.

He wiped his hands, damp with perspiration, against the sides of his trousers, then finally approached the massive front door with its intricate inlay of stained-glass flowers. He twisted the dead bolt and pulled on the wrought-iron handle.

The door swung open to reveal a casually dressed

man and woman, both around thirty. Anxiously he checked the expression in their eyes and was relieved when he saw no hint of sympathy.

He listened as they introduced themselves, then asked what he could do for them.

"There was a traffic accident yesterday afternoon on Pacific Coast Highway."

Wallace recalled seeing footage on the evening news of the pileup on the freeway. But what did that have to do with him? "Yes. A sedan caught on fire, then a tractor-trailer overturned. Terrible thing." Even as he spoke, his mind conjured an image of a motorcycle cop and a nurse carrying a baby to the hospital.

He searched their faces again and decided that it might have been them. Probably was. Did that mean the baby—?

No. Surely not.

"A woman was killed in the accident," the man— Officer Casey Guthrie—continued. "And we're having difficulty identifying her. She was in her early twenties, brown eyes, with long blond hair."

Guthrie paused with his description, obviously seeking some sign of recognition in Wallace's eyes. Wallace was able to give him none.

"Any reason why you think I might be able to help?" he asked.

"Yes. She had your address in the car with her. We believe she may have been heading here when she had the accident." He paused. "There was a two-month-old baby girl in the back seat with her."

Now the officer got the reaction he seemed to have been looking for.

Wallace couldn't help himself. *They were asking about the baby. Perhaps it was possible then.* His mouth dropped open, his heart hammered against his rib cage. "The baby—is she okay?"

Guthrie nodded, and this time it was the woman who responded. "She's at Courage Bay Hospital. One of her eyes was damaged by some broken glass. The pediatric surgeon operated almost as soon as we delivered her to the hospital. Her prognosis isn't certain at this time, but we're all hoping for the best."

"The problem now," the cop continued, "is that we're having trouble identifying her and her mother. There was no purse, wallet or papers of any kind found in the car."

Wallace sensed his family crowding up behind him. He'd have preferred that they stay in the background and let him handle this. But under the circumstances, he couldn't blame them.

It sounded to him as if they might just have had the biggest stroke of luck. "The woman is dead?" he asked, wanting to be sure about that. "And the baby is okay?"

The nurse nodded.

"Don't say 'the baby,' Wallace. It's got to be Haley. I'm sure it's Haley." He felt his wife's fingertips press into his shoulder as she leaned in closer.

"Excuse me," the nurse said, looking confused. "But who is Haley?"

"That's our granddaughter." Wallace shot a withering glance back at Abigail, warning her to be quiet. He had to be very careful what he said right now. If this dead woman was who he thought she was, his family's future could well depend on the way he handled this situation.

"Our two-month-old granddaughter has been missing for a couple of days," he continued.

Casey Guthrie looked skeptical. "How does a two-month-old baby go missing?"

"She was kidnapped, young man," Abigail said, despite her husband's warning glare. "Thank goodness you finally found her!"

CHAPTER SIX

KIDNAPPED? Casey could never have expected this. He felt Jackie's hand land on his shoulder as if she needed to steady herself. Without taking his eyes from Abigail Voltz's face, he slipped his arm around her waist.

"That's a pretty serious accusation, ma'am." Yet Abigail Voltz's expression, and indeed, that of her husband and presumably the baby's parents behind him, bore testimony to what she'd said. "Have you reported this to the police?"

"Of course not," the young man behind Abigail snapped. "Do you think we wanted them to kill her?"

"Calm down, son," Wallace said sharply. "And watch your tongue. All of you." He turned back to Casey. "My wife spoke out of turn there, Officer. We were worried that Haley had been kidnapped, but we didn't know for sure. See, my son hired a new baby-sitter. She was supposed to take Haley for a long walk so Sherri-Ann could catch up on her sleep. When she didn't return, we feared the worst."

"Did you receive any communication from this woman that might lead you to believe she was being held for ransom?" Casey asked. "Were you warned not to talk to the police?"

"No," Wallace said quickly. "We just panicked and overreacted. When you're part of a family with a lot of money, Officer Guthrie, you tend to be a little suspicious about people's motives."

"Doesn't sound like overreacting to me. You say the baby-sitter was supposed to be gone a couple of hours, but in fact had your granddaughter for several days?"

"Just one night," Wallace corrected quickly. "And there may have been some ambiguity with my son's instructions."

Casey exchanged a doubtful glance with Jackie. They were getting nothing but lies here and he could tell Jackie thought the same thing.

The rest of the Voltz family stood mutely behind Wallace, though. Casey could tell there were some differences of opinion here, but right now no one was openly defying the head of the household.

"The important thing," Wallace said, "is that Haley is fine. Nothing else matters." He seemed to be speaking more to his family than to Casey and Jackie.

"We need to go get her, Wallace," Abigail said. "Right away."

"I have her birth certificate in my purse," the daughter-in-law said. "Do you think we'll need anything else?"

"One minute." Wallace put up his hand. "We don't know for sure that this baby is Haley. If it isn't—

well, we can't all leave the house. What if that woman—the, um, baby-sitter—tries to call while we're out?"

"That baby-sitter," Casey said. "What was her name?"

Wallace blinked rapidly. "You said Susan, didn't you, Bill? Susan Smith?"

Bill stared blankly at his father, then nodded slowly. "Yeah, I think that was it."

"My son should have asked for references. Should have checked her out. She claimed to be with a reputable agency. But later, when we called the agency, they said they'd never heard of her."

More lies? It was hard to tell, but Casey asked for the name of the agency and resolved to follow up that part of their story at least.

As he scribbled the information into his notebook, he couldn't help but wonder what the hell the Voltz family was trying to hide?

"What did this Susan Smith look like?"

Bill's gaze shifted from Casey to his father, then back. "I can't really remember. I only saw her that once, and so briefly."

Did he know how unbelievable that sounded? "Hair color? Eyes?"

"She…she was wearing a hat. And sunglasses."

Casey sighed. Maybe he was getting ahead of himself here. "I guess our first step should be to figure out whether the baby we have in the hospital really is your Haley. We can sort the rest of the story out later."

"I agree. And I don't care what you say, Father, Sherri-Ann and I are going to the hospital to get her." Despite his attempt to sound authoritative, Wallace Voltz's son appeared more like a rebellious teenager than a grown man as he faced off against his dad. He was the shorter of the two, a little pudgy, with an odd cowlick above his forehead.

"Don't be a fool, Bill. You can't leave the phone." Wallace turned back to Casey and Jackie. "I'll take Sherri-Ann to the hospital right now. If it's Haley," he told his wife and son, "we'll let you know right away."

"I WONDER WHO'S THE BOSS in that family," Jackie commented as she and Casey sped back to Courage Bay Hospital. They took time to zip through a fast-food joint to grab large coffees. Lack of sleep was wearing on them both.

"Interesting family dynamics." Casey tore away the tab from the plastic cover on his cup.

"I wonder if there's any chance the baby isn't Haley Voltz." Jackie wasn't sure she wanted that obviously dysfunctional family to belong to the sweet baby she'd helped rescue. "The whole lot of them are liars, I'd bet money on that."

"You'd think they could have come up with a better story. Who lets a near stranger take their two-month-old baby out of their house? And Susan Smith—" Casey snorted. "The name's so obviously phony I almost had to laugh in their faces."

"He made it up on the spot." Jackie leaned forward in her seat anxiously. "Can't you drive a little faster? I don't want Voltz to get to Janey before we do."

Wallace, who was driving a stunning burgundy Rolls-Royce Corniche with deep tan interior, quite possibly the most beautiful convertible Casey had ever seen, hadn't stopped for coffee and so had a lead on them.

Casey glanced at the digital time display on the dash. "I'm a traffic cop, Jackie." Still, he put just a little more weight on the accelerator. He couldn't wait to get there, either.

WALLACE VOLTZ HAD JUST stepped up to the nursing station in the pediatric wing when Casey and Jackie reached the third floor, coffees in hand.

"I'm here to inquire about the baby that was in the car accident," Wallace Voltz said to the nurse sitting behind the desk.

"Janey Doe?" The nurse's gaze drifted over to Casey. Apparently she recognized him from the newscast, or maybe from hospital gossip, because she said, "Have we found the family, Officer Guthrie?"

"Not sure yet, Brenda." He read her name from the tag on her uniform. "Would it be okay if we let Mr. Voltz have a peek at her?"

"Absolutely."

They followed the nurse to the room Casey and Jackie had visited several hours earlier that morning. Haley was fussing this time, probably bothered by the bandage over her eye.

"It's her!" Wallace rushed for the infant and gathered her into his arms before anyone could intervene. Haley quieted right away, but that didn't mean anything. She'd been good when Casey had held her earlier.

"Can you be sure?" he asked the older man. "Even with the bandage on her eye?"

"I know my granddaughter when I see her, Officer Guthrie."

"Yes, that's Haley," Sherri-Ann said, holding out her arms toward the baby. After a brief hesitation, Wallace Voltz passed over his granddaughter. His gaze shifted to the nurse. "You can check your own records if you want. Haley was born here and we have her birth certificate with us."

"I'll pull the records," the nurse said. "But we won't be able to release the baby without consulting the police. I'll call them right now."

It took a while for Haley's identification to be confirmed. A decision to perform DNA testing was reversed when Wallace Voltz had both the family doctor and Haley's pediatrician positively identify the child to police. Haley had been in for her eight-week checkup just ten days ago, and her doctor recalled the distinctive birthmark on the child's left thigh.

Finally there was no doubt. Janey Doe really was Haley Abigail Voltz.

After phoning his family with the happy news, Wallace demanded to speak to the doctor who'd performed Haley's surgery. When he heard that Haley's pressure patch was ready to be replaced with a simple eye dressing, and that her prognosis was looking very good, he insisted on taking her home.

"That's impossible," the doctor told him. "Your granddaughter has just had surgery."

But Wallace Voltz wasn't a man easily dissuaded. "What if I hire a nurse?"

"Well, maybe we could discharge her tomorrow."

"How about later this afternoon?"

Listening to the exchange, Casey couldn't help but think about the baby. He and Jackie had thought her mother was dead, but it turned out she wasn't. Haley had a mom and a dad and grandparents, too. It should have been the perfect happy ending.

But as Casey watched the baby's grandfather stand guard by her bassinette, he felt a residual anxiety. From the way Jackie was chewing the gloss off her bottom lip, he knew she shared his concern. He ushered Jackie out into the hall.

"I'm sure the baby is his granddaughter," he said quietly. "But something about this setup doesn't feel right. While we were waiting for the doctor and you were in the washroom, I told Voltz we needed to go over the facts of Haley's disappearance again. If she truly was kidnapped, he needs to file an official report. I offered to take him to the police station myself, but he brushed me off."

Jackie sighed. "Maybe we should give them the benefit of the doubt. I'm sure they're all very anxious to get Haley home as soon as possible."

Jackie could well be right, but she didn't sound convinced, either.

They took their time on the stairs down to the main floor. By the time they were out on the street again, Casey realized that despite the jolt of caffeine, he was utterly exhausted.

"Home, James," Jackie said, sliding into the passenger seat of his car.

"Damn good idea." He was too tired to talk as he drove. He needed his remaining energy reserves to deal with the traffic. By the time he escorted Jackie to the door of her condo unit, Casey could tell she was as anxious as he was to hit the sheets.

"One minute," he said before she closed the door. "We haven't set a time for our next date..."

She smiled wearily. "*Next* date. We haven't had the first one, have we?"

"Pizza qualifies. Our second date will be a proper meal in a proper restaurant." He glanced at his watch. It was almost noon. "Will six hours' sleep be enough?"

"No," she said. "But if we want to sleep tonight and get back into a regular routine, it will have to do."

"Okay, so I'll see you at six." He watched her slip in the door, then, at the last second, stopped her with a touch on the shoulder.

She turned with a question in her eyes and he kissed her on the mouth so quickly she had no chance to object.

"Good night, Jackie Kellison. I'm *really* glad I met you."

TOO SHORT, Jackie thought, contemplating Casey's kiss as she headed for her bedroom, shedding clothing as she went. Once in the room, she slipped into a pair of boxer shorts and a tank top, then sank to her bed.

Heaven.

No, heaven would be the moment when she and Casey had a proper kiss, but right now she was too exhausted to even dream about that possibility.

It would happen soon enough, she told herself, if they really were going out to dinner tonight. She couldn't believe she'd accepted a date with Casey Guthrie. He couldn't be the right guy for her, no matter how much she'd enjoyed being with him today. She loved that he thought and acted quickly, that his mind seemed to operate on the same level as hers. They'd just said goodbye and already she missed him.

Not a good sign.

She should phone him and tell him she'd changed her mind. She didn't have his number, but she could leave a message for him at the police station.

But I don't want to cancel.

Jackie cuddled into her blankets. Memories of Andrew threatened, but she pushed them away.

Too tired, she thought. And that was the last moment of consciousness she remembered.

AFTER FOUR HOURS of sleep, Casey woke with a headache, a dry throat and a smile on his face. In two hours he would see Jackie Kellison again. He felt like phoning to tell her he was thinking of her, but she would likely still be sleeping, as he ought to be.

Strange how he'd been roused so early despite his exhaustion. Maybe it was the noise of the kids playing on the street below him. He'd fallen asleep with his window wide open to catch the fresh autumn breeze.

He glanced at his phone, then wished he hadn't. The message button was still flashing. He'd ignored it earlier, but now he reached over to hit the playback button. First his brother's voice filled his bedroom. Adam had seen the news, the clip of him, Jackie and the baby on his bike.

"Pretty dramatic, Casey. Don't you think it would have been safer to transport the baby in an ambulance?"

That was Adam for you. Casey folded his hands behind his head and stared up at the ceiling. The next message was from one of his buddies.

"We're going to shoot some pool over at the Bar and Grill tonight. I know you're off duty, so give me a call."

Casey scowled. What had possessed him to press that play button? With another jab of the finger he deleted both messages. Adam's slight dig didn't deserve a response. As for his buddy...well, he should probably call back, but he didn't feel up to fending off the ribald comments he knew he'd get when he explained that he had a date lined up for tonight.

Usually he handled the teasing of his mates with

ease. The arrival of each new girl in his life was acknowledged with sly winks and secret smiles. His buddies knew the score, and so did the women. Casey never pretended to be serious. If fun was on the lady's agenda, then he was more than happy to oblige until such time as fun was no longer enough.

With each girlfriend, that moment was reached sooner or later.

But even though they'd only had their first date— sort of—he already knew Jackie was different.

He couldn't pinpoint when he'd figured that out. For sure when he'd observed her in operation at the hospital, giving her all when she could easily have begged off with her own injury. Probably even sooner, when she'd been so amazingly cool and capable at the collision scene. But now he wondered if he hadn't sensed something special about her the first moment he'd spotted her whizzing past him in her bright red convertible.

The convertible that was now just a hunk of metal in a junk heap somewhere.

If she'd been driving a few miles an hour faster, it could have been her car under that rig, not the Taurus. He'd never have met her. Even just contemplating the possibility that she could have been hurt, or killed, made him desperate to see her again. Soon.

Unable to loll around in bed any longer, he went to the bathroom to shower and shave. As warm, soapy water streamed over his body, he felt cleansed in a more profound way. This day would mark the beginning of something new, a fresh chapter. The change involved Jackie Kellison, but it was more than just that.

With the clarity of hindsight, he could see that he'd been preparing to head in a different direction for a while now. He enjoyed his job and his carefree lifestyle, but the rules and regulations of police work chafed at him. He wanted a career he could really sink his teeth into, but he also wanted to run things his own way.

As for his no-strings-attached policy where women were concerned, he was tired of that, as well. Maybe turning thirty had brought about this change in him. Or maybe he simply hadn't met the right woman until now.

With his brother, Adam, and his fiancée, Faith, love had been a one-shot deal. Now that he'd met Jackie Kellison, Casey had a feeling it was going to be the same for him.

SOMETHING'S DIFFERENT...

Jackie opened her eyes and peered out at her familiar bedroom. Her neck ached, but that wasn't what troubled her. She thought about the accident and her totaled car. Her vague concerns about Haley and the puzzling facts of her separation from her family. All those things worried Jackie, but she knew they didn't explain why she had woken from a deep sleep with a feeling straddling anticipation and apprehension.

She glanced at her bedside alarm and the thought came that she had two hours before she'd agreed to meet Casey Guthrie for dinner. *Casey.* Immediately she knew that the motorcycle patrol officer was the reason she'd awoken feeling so unsettled.

Time to date again. All the important people in her life kept telling her that, and she knew they were right, that she was healed and ready. But she was dead certain Casey Guthrie wasn't the man to start with.

He was good-looking, yes. Maybe too good-looking. Charming, as well, but again, maybe too charming. If Kell and Nate were right, and Casey was used to dating lots of pretty women, how long would his interest in her last?

He'd made it clear that he'd been impressed with the way she'd handled herself at the accident scene. What he couldn't appreciate was that any trained ER nurse would have reacted the same way. She wasn't a hero, and she wasn't especially brave, either.

Maybe once long ago she'd been brash and bold and unstoppable. But that had been before Andrew. If Casey believed she was that sort of woman, he was bound to be disappointed.

Jackie slid out of bed and headed for the living room. Her wedding photo in its silver frame, once prominently displayed on her coffee table, was now tucked behind a vase filled with pretty pieces of cut glass. She pulled it out and braced herself for the jolt of pain she always felt when she looked back into the past this way.

She'd been so happy on her wedding day, and

Andrew had seemed almost effervescent. You could see it in the photograph: his overbright eyes and full-wattage smile. She hadn't realized then what she understood now. That Andrew's hyper, almost-manic high was symptomatic of mood swings that would see him crashing in a matter of days, or sometimes even hours.

Poor Andrew. I never really knew you, did I? She of all people, a trained nurse, had missed the most obvious symptoms, probably, she now realized, because she'd been in denial.

It was time to pack this away, Jackie decided, setting the heavy frame on the table next to the sofa. Later, she'd get the box where she kept all her keepsakes out of storage and add this picture to the collection.

She felt good about the decision. The timing felt right. Just as it had for her decision, several months ago, to stop wearing her wedding ring.

Jackie showered, then dressed in a flowered skirt and plain-colored silk T-shirt, before drying light curls into the feathered layers of her hair. As she fastened the clasp on her watch, she noted that more than an hour remained until she was supposed to meet Casey.

She would go on this date with him, since she'd more or less agreed to. But it would be their last. Then she'd start looking for that accountant. Or maybe, having had one pseudo-date with Casey, she could skip right ahead to the dentist.

Rather than wait around her apartment, she decided to go to the hospital to check on Haley. Then she remembered she didn't have a car anymore, which was a minor annoyance. She'd called her insurance company earlier to report the accident but still needed to arrange a rental to tide her over until she bought something new.

This afternoon she splurged on a cab. She waited on the street for the driver to show up, then hopped in the back seat. "Courage Bay Hospital, please."

Their route took them onto the Pacific Coast Highway, of course, and as they cruised past the accident scene, Jackie shivered. The highway had been cleared of all the damaged vehicles. All she could see to indicate the tragedy of little more than twenty-four hours ago were several dark skid marks.

She'd been so lucky. What was a little whiplash and a totaled vehicle compared with what others had suffered? She thought about the man in the sedan and the woman—Susan Smith?—who'd been driving the Taurus. Was it really possible that woman had been a kidnapper?

It seemed far-fetched, but so did the Voltzes' story about leaving their baby with a baby-sitter they didn't know. The only fact Jackie felt she could be certain of was that the baby did belong to Bill and Sherri-Ann Voltz. The baby's footprint had matched the one taken at birth, and the strawberry-colored mark on her thigh had been verified by the pediatrician.

So why did the thought of those people taking Haley fill Jackie with trepidation? The Voltzes must be good parents. No question that until the day of the accident, the baby had been well cared for. She was plump and alert for her age—her skin healthy and pink.

Jackie had the cab drop her off outside the main entrance of the hospital. She'd paid her fare and was just stepping out to the paved sidewalk when she heard her name.

"Jackie?"

It was Casey. He stood to the side of the entrance, dressed in jeans and a cotton shirt. Seeing him unexpectedly like this threw her entire system into overload. Her heart beat too hard and too fast. Her skin went hot. Her breathing sped up.

He was so attractive. Any woman would be thrilled to be the recipient of that smile. She couldn't stop herself from smiling in return. She wished he would rush toward her, maybe even give her a little hug or a kiss, but he held a cell phone in his hand. Holding out his palm in a gesture for her to wait, he resumed speaking.

As he paced down the sidewalk, she heard him raise his voice, then shake his head. He turned and began to stride in the opposite direction, toward the hospital. "Are you sure?" he asked. Then a minute later he asked the same question again.

It didn't occur to her that his conversation could have anything to do with her. She assumed he was discussing a personal matter. She knew nothing about his life. Perhaps there was a woman. Someone he'd been seeing before he'd met her. Someone he was *still* seeing.

"Well, that's that, I guess." Casey shut his cell phone and stuffed it into the pocket of his jeans.

"What's the problem?"

"Oh—it's complicated. What are you doing here, Jackie?" He glanced at his watch. "Aren't you supposed to be sleeping?"

Never in a million years would she admit that he was the reason she'd woken early. "I couldn't stop worrying about Haley. I'm going to run up and check on her."

"She isn't here, Jackie. That's why I came, too. But Haley's gone. She was discharged an hour ago."

Jackie was floored by disappointment. She'd wanted—no, she'd *needed*—to say goodbye to that little sweetie. "So soon?"

"Apparently, Wallace Voltz was adamant about taking her home. According to the nurses, he wouldn't leave her alone for a second."

"Do you think he was afraid she might be kidnapped again?" Assuming she'd been kidnapped the first time. But the more Jackie thought about the situation, the more she felt that was exactly what had happened. "Maybe the police should be sent to question the family."

"They already have. I phoned my brother on my way home from your place. I told him what had happened and he sent a couple of detectives to the house."

"And?"

"I just finished talking to him. He says the family is standing by their story that they'd merely left the baby with a new baby-sitter. They're going to check out the Susan Smith angle, but with a name like that, we'll never get anywhere."

"What about the agency Wallace claimed he called?"

"I've already questioned them. They had no Susan Smith in their employ. And no one there remembers anyone from the Voltz family phoning to question them about her."

"So the entire story was fabricated."

"I think we both knew that."

She nodded. "When we first arrived at the house, Abigail said Haley was kidnapped."

"Apparently she has retracted that statement. Her husband says she tends to be flighty when she's under stress."

Jackie looked around and saw that at some point in their conversation, she and Casey had settled on one of the wrought-iron benches that flanked the hospital entrance. She kicked at the crushed rock beneath her feet. "I don't buy that. The Voltzes are hiding something. But why would they want to protect the woman who kidnapped their granddaughter?"

"Exactly what worries me. Before, when the kidnapper had the baby and might possibly have hurt her, there was reason to keep silent. But Haley's back with her family now."

"Yes. I wish I could feel better about that."

"So you feel uneasy, too?"

Jackie swallowed. "Absolutely. Oh, Casey. Do you think Haley's going to be all right?"

"I wish I could say yes. But what if Susan Smith had a partner?"

"Oh, Lord, I never thought of that."

"I think it's pretty likely. We've run the woman's fingerprints through our system and we've come up with nothing. Susan Smith—if that really is her name—has no criminal record. Not the sort of woman you can imagine planning a kidnapping on her own. Not to mention grand auto theft."

"That's a good point."

"You know what I find really irritating? You and I *know* something is fishy here, yet the police department can't do anything. Without any evidence of a crime, or a statement from a member of the Voltz family, we have no justification for conducting an investigation."

"Why do I sense your frustration with the police department goes deeper than this one case?"

"I don't hide my emotions very well, do I? My brother is always on my back about that. A police officer keeps his composure at all times. He is impartial and fair…but damn it, when you know a guy is guilty, the rules and regulations can drive you crazy."

"I understand. We run up against the same problems in the ER. Patients who need help but don't have insurance. Parents that you *know* are abusive, but you have to let their injured children go home with them because you haven't got enough evidence to take them away…" At times she felt her heart would break, but then there were days like yesterday, when she believed she was making a difference.

They sat in silence for a couple of minutes, lost in their thoughts. Then Jackie noticed a woman approach from down the street. She was about forty, tall and slender, dressed in an elegant business suit, her cinnamon-colored hair swept up off her fine-featured face. It was Callie Baker, the chief of staff at Courage Bay Hospital and Jackie's ultimate superior.

Callie was walking quickly, her expression distracted. She'd triggered the automatic opening of the hospital's glass doors before she noticed Jackie and Casey on the nearby bench.

"Jackie Kellison?" She stopped short and swung around.

The two women saw each other routinely at staff meetings, but had never had a personal conversation before. Jackie hadn't expected Callie to know her name.

"Yes, Dr. Baker." She stood, respectfully. Callie was intensely committed to her job. She demanded a lot from her staff, but she was fair, too. Jackie considered herself lucky to work for the woman.

"I saw the news yesterday." Callie noticed Casey then, as he raised himself from the bench to stand at Jackie's side. She gave him a brief nod. "You must be Officer Guthrie. That was quite a job you two did yesterday."

Jackie couldn't tell how Dr. Baker meant her comment. "I suppose we should have waited for the ambulance. But I was worried about permanent damage to the baby's eye. A piece of glass had perforated her cornea—"

Callie silenced her with a gesture. "Why don't you come up to my office now? I've been meaning to talk to you about this."

CHAPTER SEVEN

JACKIE HAD NEVER BEEN in Dr. Callie Baker's office before, and the first thing she noticed, besides the almost compulsive neatness, was the framed publicity photographs along the back wall. One was the same shot of Dr. Baker with Wallace and Abigail Voltz that she'd discovered in Haley's diaper bag.

Turning from the framed clipping, Jackie focused on the chief of staff, who riffled through a stack of printed messages before indicating that Jackie should sit.

With too much time to speculate on the reason for this chat, Jackie had assumed the worst. Finally she couldn't keep silent any longer.

"Is Haley Voltz okay? I heard she was discharged this afternoon."

"You know her name," Dr. Baker observed. "Yes, Haley is fine, and it's mostly thanks to you. I was speaking to her doctors earlier and their prognosis is optimistic for the complete recovery of her vision."

"Oh, thank God."

"Yes, it's very good news. I did have a call from one board member this morning who wondered about liability issues had you encountered some sort of unfortunate mishap while transporting the baby here on the motorcycle."

Jackie prepared herself for the reprimand.

"I can't officially condone the decision you made," the doctor continued. "At the same time, I can't help but see you as a hero. Hospital administration can't spell out the rules for every possible emergency situation our staff will encounter. But I can only hope that all my nurses would react with the sort of clear thinking and, yes, bravery that you exhibited.

"And I'm not only talking about the baby, Jackie. You helped many people yesterday, and don't think your efforts weren't noticed. And appreciated."

With that, she stood and handed over the stack of messages that Jackie had assumed were Dr. Baker's. Skimming the top one, Jackie realized it was a thank-you e-mail from the mother of the boy she'd assisted right after the accident occurred.

"I understand you're on four days off right now."

"Yes."

"Well, let's make that a week. Extra paid leave. I notice you're holding your neck a little stiffly. You need to take care of yourself. I recommend a physio assessment and lots of rest and relaxation for the next few days."

Finally, Jackie broke out a smile. She was being *commended*. Not reprimanded. "Thank you, Dr. Baker."

"Thank *you*, Jackie. And you can pass on my

thanks to Officer Guthrie, as well." Callie Baker's smile turned a little playful. "My guess is you're going to be seeing a lot of that fellow in the near future."

CASEY WAS WAITING for Jackie when she emerged from the hospital and her unexpected meeting with Dr. Baker. He could tell that she was shaken by something, and when he touched her shoulder, she passed him a sheaf of papers.

"Look at these," she said weakly.

They sat on the bench again and read through the pile of grateful messages from several of the victims Jackie had helped at the scene of the accident. When they were done, Casey felt something strong and sure rise up inside him. He wanted to hug her, but didn't think she was ready for that. Instead he squeezed her hand.

"These are wonderful."

"Yes."

"Now do you believe me when I call you a hero? All these people—"

She didn't let him finish his sentence. "No. Please, Casey, don't call me that. I'm just a nurse, trained to deal with emergency situations. That's all."

He could understand her reticence to take credit for what she'd done. But he couldn't believe she didn't see herself the way he did. As brave and, well, incredible. And not only at the collision scene. Even today she'd struck him as tenacious, bright and headstrong.

Why did she refuse to acknowledge these qualities in herself?

"What time is it, Casey?"

He glanced at his watch. "Time for me to pick you up for our date. Are you hungry?"

"I could eat," she said, "but I'd feel better if I knew Haley was all right. Do you think we could drop over to Bill and Sherri-Ann's house to check out the situation?"

"I've been toying with the idea myself. But it occurs to me that they might not be very happy to see us."

"We're the ones who saved their daughter," she reminded him. "Really, they ought to be more grateful, don't you think?"

"Oh, absolutely."

They both laughed. Casey was amazed at how often he and Jackie were on the same wavelength. Maybe he was reading too much into too little. After all, they'd known each other barely twenty-four hours.

But he didn't think he was. They had a special connection. And right now he was pretty sure that Jackie was aware of it, too.

THEY FOUND Bill Voltz's address in the phone book. He lived miles from his father's seaside mansion, in a modest bungalow with a double garage and a patchy garden. Bill Voltz was out cutting the lawn when they pulled up in front of his house, his cowlick more pronounced than ever in his sweat-dampened hair.

"Hmm." Casey contemplated the home and the man in the front yard. He checked Jackie's expression for her impression.

"In a different class altogether from Daddy."

"Just what I was thinking." A stroller had been left at the side door. He watched as the younger Voltz kicked it out of the way to continue trimming an inch of growth from his shabby-looking lawn.

Jackie gripped the car's door handle. "Do you think he'll be okay with us showing up like this?"

"Oh, sure. He'll probably offer us a handsome reward for saving his daughter's eyesight."

They were both chuckling over this as they emerged from the car. It was past the dinner hour and soon would be dark. They'd abandoned their plans for a leisurely meal at a pricey restaurant and instead had stopped for tacos on the way over.

Could the tacos count as their second date? Casey was afraid his plans to wine and dine Jackie had fallen off the rails. But their worry about Haley preempted all other concerns right now.

Bill Voltz did not look welcoming as he stood, hands on hips, and watched them approach. He'd switched off the lawn mower and the sudden silence was unnerving.

"Didn't expect to see you two again."

"You remember us then." Casey grinned as if he was becoming reacquainted with an old friend.

"Oh, I remember." Bill nodded at Jackie. "Ms. Kellison."

"Jackie, please."

Bill nodded again, then adjusted his head slightly to the right. "And Officer Guthrie."

"Casey. I'm off duty, here on a personal visit

only." He wanted to make that perfectly clear, hoping the young Voltz couple might be disarmed and say more than they intended.

With this in mind, Casey made an appreciative comment about the All Road Quattro Audi visible through the open garage door. Though Bill's house and property were decidedly middle class, the man had obviously splurged on his vehicle. "That's a beauty. Looks new."

"It is something, isn't it?" Bill's expression softened. "Want to take a look?"

Whether Jackie was interested in cars or not, she listened as raptly as Casey while Bill extolled the virtues of his new car. She ran a hand over the hood appreciatively. "I wish I could afford to replace my banged-up convertible with one of these."

Casey suspected she wished nothing of the sort, but Bill seemed flattered.

"Yeah, it's pretty costly. My old man wanted only the best for his granddaughter. You should hear the safety features…"

They spent fifteen minutes in the garage, then finally Bill said, "I should thank you both for your part in saving Haley. My wife and I really are grateful our daughter wasn't injured any worse than she was. The doctors hope she'll recover her eyesight completely."

Casey wondered if Jackie found Bill's professed gratitude as phony as he did. He glanced at her and saw the skepticism in her eyes.

"I'm glad you mentioned Haley," Casey said. "Because that's why we're here. Jackie and I became quite attached to her, and we were surprised when we heard she'd already been discharged. If it isn't inconvenient, we'd like to visit her one more time."

"Normally I'd say yes, no problem." Bill glanced back at the house uncertainly. "But we're trying to establish some routine in Haley's life again. I think Sherri-Ann is putting her to sleep right now."

"Didn't I hear your father say he was going to hire a private nurse?"

"Oh, well, she's gone to the drugstore to get some prescriptions filled. I tell you, they're giving my kid way too many drugs in my opinion."

"Anytime you have surgery, there's a chance of infection. It's important that Haley be given all her medication," Jackie reminded him.

She frowned at Casey again. He wondered if she suspected the same thing he did, that Bill Voltz had dismissed the nurse. But why?

"Perhaps we could visit Haley at a more convenient time," Casey suggested. "Would tomorrow work?"

"I'm not sure. Like Jackie just said, Haley needs to recover from her surgery."

"How about Friday, then?"

Casey's persistence paid off. "I suppose a short visit couldn't hurt. Late afternoon is usually the best. Haley naps from about two until four. So around five o'clock?"

"Okay then. Friday at five."

Bill glanced pointedly at Casey's car, expecting

them to head off. But Jackie's stubborn expression told Casey she was reluctant to leave without at least one glimpse of Haley.

But what could he do? He had no legal right to force Bill to show him his daughter.

Then the front door opened unexpectedly and Sherri-Ann appeared on the stoop.

Since they were standing in the shadow of the garage, the petite redhead didn't see them at first. "Bill? Have you finally finished the damn lawn?"

The three of them stepped out into full view and Sherri-Ann reacted with a visible jolt of surprise. Her hair was pulled back in a ponytail, and with her blotchy skin and puffy eyes, she looked very young and very unhappy.

"Sweetheart?" Bill said. From her blank gaze, she didn't seem to realize who the visitors were. "You remember the cop and the nurse who took Haley to the hospital after the accident? Casey Guthrie and Jackie Kellison. They've come to visit Haley, but I told them Friday would be better. She's sleeping, right?"

"I just settled her down." Sherri-Ann inched back toward the house. Addressing Casey and Jackie, she managed a slight smile. "Please excuse me for being such a mess. I'm so glad to have my baby back, I can't stop crying. I know that sounds stupid, but—"

"We understand," Jackie said gently.

"We're so fortunate you were there at the right time to help Haley," she told them.

Again, the profession of gratitude didn't strike

Casey as exactly heartfelt. "How's she doing?" he asked. "Is she having any trouble with her eye?"

"It's healing just fine."

"The nurse must be a tremendous help," Casey said, interested in seeing her reaction.

She glanced quickly at her husband, and for a moment her pale eyes gleamed with anger. Then she looked back at Casey and put a hand to her throat. "Yes."

Wanting to prod further, he said the first thing he could think of. "Your father sure seemed anxious when we were at the hospital. I guess he's really close to his granddaughter."

This time it was Bill's expression that revealed anger. And resentment, too. "The only thing my father is really close to is his money."

"Technically, it isn't even his money," Sherri-Ann pointed out. "It's your mom's."

"Doesn't matter. Dad has always controlled the purse strings. And he's always been a tightwad. When it comes to family, anyway."

"Face it, Bill. He uses his power over the money to control you. Of course, when it comes to charity, it's a different story. He has quite a reputation for philanthropy in this town. I guess he's never heard the saying 'Charity begins at home.' I mean, look at this place." With a sweep of her arm, Sherri-Ann indicated the house behind her. "Compared to the way my in-laws live, this is a hovel. You'd think he'd want something nicer for his only grandchild."

The place seemed comfortable enough to Casey,

but if Sherri-Ann had been expecting to live in a mansion like the Voltzes when she married Bill, he could see why she'd be disappointed.

While talking to Sherri-Ann, he and Jackie had made their way to the front door.

"Could I just take a quick peek at Haley?" Jackie asked. "She's such a sweetie. I promise I won't wake her."

Casey had to admire her persistence, and this time it paid off. Though she frowned, Sherri-Ann did step back and allow him and Jackie access to the house.

"It's that room on the right." She pointed down the hall.

Casey had a quick impression of pink walls, the scent of baby powder and a sleeping infant. Then Sherri-Ann was ushering them back outside. Bill had put away the lawn mower and was locking his Audi.

Casey wondered if money was the source of the problem here. If Haley had been kidnapped, perhaps Wallace Voltz had refused to pay ransom. Could that be why this young couple seemed so resentful?

But there was more than resentment toward Wallace at play. Sherri-Ann was obviously furious with Bill about something. Getting rid of the nurse, if indeed that was what had happened? Whatever the source of Sherri-Ann's ire, Bill seemed to be doing his best to appease her. Casey wasn't interested in the ordinary tribulations of a married couple. But he had the feeling that somehow their dispute involved Haley.

This visit had been meant to reassure him and Jackie that the little girl was all right. But despite having seen the infant asleep in her crib, he felt more worried about her than ever.

CHAPTER EIGHT

SINCE THE ACCIDENT, Jackie's internal clock had gone haywire. When Casey stood in the hall in front of her apartment door, having driven her home from Bill and Sherri-Ann's, she had the disorienting sensation of not knowing whether it was morning or night. She glanced at her watch.

"Nine o'clock. That's in the evening, right?"

Casey seemed amused. "Tell me that I'm the reason your head is in the clouds." He took a step closer, rested his forearm against the door frame.

He was part of the reason. Maybe the main one. Jackie didn't think it was wise to admit it, though. "It's always hard coming off a night shift."

"Anything I can do to make it easier?"

His tone remained teasing, but there was a serious look in his eyes, too. Given his reputation and the short time she'd known him, Jackie wondered why she had the feeling that she could count on this man. If she were ever in trouble, she would be able to turn to him. To lean on him.

Something she'd never been able to do with Andrew.

"Still hurts, does it?"

For a second she thought he was talking about her former husband, then she realized she'd been rubbing the aching muscles in her neck.

"You should probably get that looked at."

Callie Baker had said the same thing. Jackie knew they were both right, but a little whiplash didn't seem too important right now. "Maybe tomorrow."

"I'm going to see that you do," Casey promised.

Another overprotective male. Added to her brothers, it should have been the last thing she wanted. But Casey's concern didn't feel like a burden at all, more like a welcome safety net.

Despite her reservations about the man, she found herself asking, "Would you like a cup of coffee?"

"Oh, yeah. I would. I really would."

He was inside the apartment before she knew it, closing the door, twisting the dead bolt.

"That's a lot of enthusiasm for a cup of coffee."

He winked. "I have a feeling you make good coffee."

Though she hadn't dated in a long while, Jackie was pretty sure they weren't really talking about coffee. Regardless, she went to the kitchen and put on a pot, all the time wondering at the twist of fate that had brought such a sexy, charming guy into her life.

When was he going to realize she wasn't his type? Would the disappointment come with the coffee…or later?

"So what did you think of Bill and Sherri-Ann?"

Casey was in the adjacent living room, casually

perusing her bookshelves. She remembered he'd been drawn to them the last time he was here, too.

"I'm not sure," she said to answer his question. "Did you notice the tension between them? I wonder what they'd been fighting about. Their only point of agreement seems to be resenting his father."

"No kidding. That came across loud and clear, didn't it? Thank God my parents aren't rich. I'm not so sure growing up around money is an advantage."

"Do they live in Courage Bay, your parents?"

"They do, though they're on a big holiday in Europe right now. My brother and I have lived here all our lives. How about you?"

"Same." While the coffee brewed, Jackie sat on the sofa to wait. "In fact, one of our ancestors was the first officer of the *Ranger*. You're familiar with the history, I assume?"

Most kids who grew up in Courage Bay knew that the city had been founded about a century and a half earlier, when the crew members aboard the American ship *Ranger* were rescued by the local Indians. Many of the shipwrecked sailors ended up settling in the area, falling in love with the beautiful Indian maidens and raising families.

"That's a heritage to be proud of." Casey joined her on the sofa, strategically choosing a point close enough but not too close to make her uncomfortable. "Do your parents still live here?"

"They died in a car accident when I was very young. My brothers and I were raised by our grandfather on a quarter-horse ranch just outside the city limits. Then when Grandpa died, Kell looked after Nate and me. I owe a lot to my brothers."

"They must be great guys. I've seen Kell at the station, but we've never worked together."

"He's only working mounted patrol part-time now. Mostly he runs the family ranch, Whispering Dawn."

"Is that where that picture was taken?" Casey pointed to a photograph from last summer.

"Yes. That's Kell's horse, Butter, in the background."

"What about your younger brother?"

"Nate's a paramedic. He was at the scene of the accident the other day."

"The tall guy with dark brown hair? I remember noticing him. So, Jackie—two big strong brothers to watch out for you." Casey put his arm across the back of the sofa and touched a strand of her hair. "How do you manage to get in any trouble?"

"I don't." Not lately. But in the past... Jackie thought wistfully of the woman she'd once been.

"Do you lead such a very exemplary life, then?"

She laughed. "Exemplary. Yeah, that's me all right."

"You didn't look so exemplary when you were speeding along the freeway the first time I saw you, doing about fifteen clicks over the limit."

She didn't even pretend to be chastened.

"You looked beautiful, though. Happy and carefree."

"That's how I felt." Then the accident had happened, and she'd been reminded how easily tragedy could mar the most beautiful of days.

"You know what I think? You're a woman who likes adventure, only you've had far too little of it lately."

"You're wrong."

"So you haven't been having fun today?"

"That hasn't been because I'm not adventurous. I'm truly worried about Haley."

"Well, so am I. But that doesn't mean I don't enjoy nosing around. And so do you."

Jackie couldn't argue anymore. The truth was, she'd felt more alive since she'd met Casey than she had in years.

"I think I'm good for you, Jackie Kellison."

No. Oh, no. Just because she felt whole and alive again didn't mean an affair with Casey was the right solution. *Second date, last date,* she reminded herself just as Casey reached across the sofa for her.

First he touched her shoulder. Then he slid closer and put his arm around her. She knew what was happening, of course.

He was going to kiss her. It was only to be expected after going out with the man—even just for tacos—then inviting him home for coffee. Jackie told herself it was okay. She was ready, she could handle this kiss. When it was over, she'd be all primed for the dentist. Maybe she'd end up marrying the dentist.

Strange how life rarely worked out as planned.

When she married Andrew, she'd never dreamed she would kiss another man. She'd promised to love her husband for better or worse, and that's what she'd done. When his mood swings had become more pronounced, when his dark days happened more frequently, she'd never once thought of turning her back on him.

For better or worse.

But Andrew was gone now, and she had to move on. She willed herself to relax as Casey came even closer. When she could feel the warmth of his skin radiating on hers, she closed her eyes. And was surprised when Casey's kiss landed not on her lips but on her cheek.

"You're nervous. You don't need to be nervous with me."

She opened her eyes and saw that he was looking at something just beyond her. Immediately she knew it was the wedding photo she'd moved off her bookshelf earlier in the day. She should have put it into storage right away.

"What was his name?" Casey asked.

"Andrew. We were married for three years." Jackie noticed her hands were tightly clenched in her lap. *Good job at relaxing, Jackie.* No wonder Casey hadn't kissed her properly.

"You don't wear a ring. Are you divorced?"

"No, not divorced." She stared straight ahead, trying to ignore the sick feeling in her stomach. "Andrew died. I'm a widow, I guess."

It was a label that had never felt right to her.

Widow suited someone older, a woman who'd lived a full life with her husband, not one who'd just been starting out in marriage.

"I'm sorry." Casey touched the bottom of her chin with a finger.

Jackie took a deep breath. *Tell him the rest,* she urged herself. She'd never have a better opening. But she couldn't make the words come.

Casey seemed to sense her struggle, and kindly he let her off the hook. "That's okay. We can talk about this later. We have lots of time, you and me. No need to rush."

He kissed her again, this time on the forehead. As he got up to leave, Jackie followed, thinking to herself he was wrong. They wouldn't have lots of time. This was going to be their last date.

After the way she'd frozen when he tried to kiss her, he'd probably be relieved. Maybe he wouldn't even ask her out again.

But he did.

"What about lunch tomorrow at the Courage Bay Bar and Grill?"

She felt a shiver of delightful anticipation.

"I'll pick you up at twelve."

He left before she could explain that a third date was out of the question.

CASEY HAD BARELY ARRIVED home when the phone rang. He picked it up, expecting it would be Adam or one of his friends.

But it was Abigail Voltz.

"Excuse me for calling you at home, Officer Guthrie. And so late."

"Is something wrong, Mrs. Voltz? Is Haley all right?"

"I'm not sure. That's why I'm calling *you*."

He waited, but she didn't seem to be in a hurry to explain. "How, exactly, can I help?"

He heard her sigh. "I should probably never have called. I thought you truly seemed to care about our granddaughter when you came to our house the other day."

"I do care about Haley," he assured her swiftly. "Is there a problem?"

"I'm afraid there might be. But first promise me you won't tell anyone what I'm about to say. Except maybe that nurse. She looks pretty and sweet, but I can tell she has a stiff backbone."

Even Abigail Voltz recognized what Jackie tried so hard to deny. "I promise," he told her.

"Haley really was kidnapped."

He'd been right.

"She was kidnapped and we paid the ransom. My husband and I liquidated three million dollars in the space of two days. It wasn't easy, let me tell you. But finally we had the money collected in a suitcase, just the way we'd been told."

"The kidnapper contacted you, not your son?"

"Yes. I guess she knew we were the ones with the money. But she wanted Bill to deliver the ransom."

"And what happened?"

"Well, he left the money where she told him, but

something went wrong and she didn't show up at the place where he was supposed to collect Haley. His father was so angry at Bill. Wallace told him he always bungles everything, which isn't fair—"

"What did Bill do then?" Casey asked, trying to refocus Abigail on the story she'd been telling.

"He went home to pick up Sherri-Ann and they drove straight to our house. Bill was certain the kidnapper would phone us again. We were waiting for the call when you arrived."

"You speak of the kidnapper as a she. Do you think there was more than one person involved?"

"That's exactly what I'm worried about. You say that woman died in the car crash. But what if she had a partner? It seems to me that Bill and Sherri-Ann aren't being very cautious. I'm terribly afraid something might happen to Haley again. After all, they got three million the first time. Why not try for more?"

Abigail Voltz's logic was frighteningly on the mark. "You need to come down to the station, Mrs. Voltz, and make a statement. I could be by in fifteen minutes to give you a ride."

"No! No, we can't do that. My husband would be furious if he knew I'd been talking to you. He thinks this is a family matter and we should handle it ourselves."

"But Haley's life could be in danger."

"Exactly so. That's why I'm calling you. I want you to find out if there was a partner in this kidnapping scheme. I need to know if Haley is still in danger. Could you do that for me, Officer Guthrie? I'd pay you very well."

"I can't accept money for that sort of work, Mrs. Voltz. I'm a member of the Courage Bay police force, not a work-for-hire investigator. Maybe you should call someone else."

"You're the only person I can trust," she insisted. "And I know you won't let Haley down. You and that lovely nurse wouldn't be hanging around my family if you didn't have the same concerns that I have."

She had him there. Abigail was much smarter— and more determined—than her appearance would indicate.

"If you tell anyone about this call, I shall deny every word. This is between *us,* Officer Guthrie. You and me. I'm asking for your help. Actually, I'm begging for it. But I can't go to the police. That is simply out of the question."

Casey raised his gaze to the ceiling and shook his head. She wasn't making this easy on him. "Can you give me any other information to go on? Something that might help me if I do decide to look into this?"

Abigail didn't get a chance to answer. "I hear footsteps. It must be Wallace. Excuse me for hanging up on you."

He heard a soft click and she was gone.

For a long moment he stood, thinking. Clearly he could not continue this investigation as a police officer. He was off duty and, furthermore, he had no information he could present to his superiors to convince them that an investigation was called for. Abigail had assured him she would deny this call if he told the authorities, and he had no doubt she would follow through on her threat.

On the other hand, to conduct his own clandestine investigation could get him in serious trouble at work. He'd stepped beyond a few boundaries in the past and had his hand slapped. This time, his very job might be at stake.

But what about Haley Voltz? Both he and Jackie felt uneasy about the baby. Now her grandmother was confirming their suspicions.

He had to do something; he couldn't live with himself otherwise. Mind made up, Casey grabbed a fresh notebook, dropped into his armchair and began jotting down his observations, starting from that first day when he and Jackie had pulled Haley from her kidnapper's wrecked car.

From memory, he reconstructed his and Jackie's first conversation with the Voltz family. Abigail Voltz had definitely stated that Haley had been kidnapped. But she'd recanted quickly once she'd found out Haley was alive and the driver of the car was dead.

Next he made notes on his and Jackie's conversation with Bill and Sherri-Ann at their house. Then, finally, he wrote, as close to word-for-word as he could manage, this last phone conversation with Abigail.

As he relived the conversation, he felt again that she'd been telling him the truth. Still, several details about her story didn't make sense.

The first discrepancy involved the exchange of money for baby. What had gone wrong? Had the kidnapper never intended to return the baby? But if that were the case, Haley would probably be dead.

Had something else gone wrong, then? The drop-off compromised? A disagreement among the kidnappers?

Which led to the next question. How many criminals were they dealing with here? For sure the dead woman in the car. He wondered most of all about her.

Who was she, and had she stolen that vehicle in order to return Haley to her family? If so, where was the ransom money? It hadn't been in the car. Every inch of the vehicle had been thoroughly inspected during the investigation of the collision.

An hour passed, maybe longer. Casey had pages of his notebook filled. Mostly with questions. Precious few answers.

It occurred to him that he enjoyed the process of collecting facts and trying to sort out solutions. Finally, he put the notebook away and caught a few hours of sleep.

First thing the next morning, he called his brother.

"Any luck identifying the woman in the car accident yet?"

"Good morning to you, too, Casey."

"Cut the pleasant chitchat, would you? People in love can be so annoying."

"You should try it sometime."

For a change, Casey didn't scoff. *Maybe he would,* he thought instead.

"What about that nurse you transported on the back of your bike the other day?"

Trust Adam to clue right in. "Her name is Jackie Kellison."

Adam laughed. "I knew it. I can tell by your voice. You've fallen for her, haven't you? When do I get to meet her?"

"I wish I could tell you." He was more intrigued by the woman than ever, but their relationship was progressing slower than he'd hoped. Last night when he'd tried to kiss Jackie, she hadn't said anything to stop him, but she'd gone all rigid in his arms. His ego wouldn't let him believe that he'd repulsed her.

"What's the matter? Is the girl not as cooperative as usual?"

"Woman. Not girl." And he didn't want to talk about her. Not yet. He was sure she felt the same attraction, the same *connection*, that he did. But she was cautious. Where he was willing to fling himself wholeheartedly into an instant love affair, she was holding back.

He didn't think it was Jackie's nature to be so guarded. Something in her past had made her that way. He wondered what it was—how bad had she been hurt? Until he knew, their relationship could only go so far.

"Enough about my love life. Give me some answers about the dead woman the city's been storing in the morgue..."

Adam released a resigned sigh. "Far as I've heard, they still don't know who she is. But don't worry. Eventually someone will report a missing person and the descriptions will match."

Yeah, yeah, yeah. And by then, Haley Voltz might have been kidnapped again. Casey wished he could tell his brother about the phone call from Abigail. But he had no doubt she would deny every word of their conversation if he put her to the test.

"I do have some interesting news that trickled in from the accident investigation," Adam said. "Remember the sedan that went up in flames? The investigation report says you noted two separate explosions."

"That's right."

"Well, that was clever of you. Nora Keyes has been looking into the incident. You know Nora? She's an expert on explosive devices."

"Sure I know her. She's a dynamite redhead."

Adam groaned. "Anyway, she figures an explosive started that fire."

"Are you kidding? That's bizarre."

"Tell me about it. Her theory is that the device was hidden in the driver's cell phone and detonated when the cell phone started to ring."

"Who was the guy in that car anyway? Sounds like he must have been bloody unpopular."

"Julius Straus. He worked as a product designer at Finder Electronics. I guess he was quite the inventor. Came up with all sorts of innovations for computer chips in internal combustion engines."

"Computer chips. That doesn't sound too controversial. Any idea why someone wanted to kill him?"

"No answers yet. But Nora is a pretty tenacious investigator. She'll figure it out eventually."

THAT SAME MORNING on the phone with Nate, Jackie compared notes on the aftermath of the collision.

"What about the woman who died, Nate? Was she…recognizable?"

"Her injuries were massive, but ironically her facial structure survived pretty much intact. When the cops find her family, they should be able to identify her okay."

"She wouldn't have suffered?"

"Death would have been instantaneous," Nate confirmed.

"It's amazing, isn't it?—that the baby survived. That her injuries weren't worse than they were."

"That Haley Voltz is one lucky child. I assume she's still at the hospital?"

"Actually, she was discharged yesterday. Casey and I are planning to visit her on Friday."

"Casey? Still seeing him are you?"

"Seeing, yes. Dating, not really. Unless you count a few stops for coffee and fast food. We've been following up the situation with the baby."

But Nate didn't seem too concerned about Haley Voltz anymore. "You haven't shared any breakfasts with this guy yet, have you?"

"Nate!"

"Well, have you?"

"You'd never put up with me grilling you about your love life like this."

"Well, forgive me, sis, but I haven't gone through what you've gone through, either. You deserve some fun in your life, don't get me wrong. But from what

Kell says, Casey Guthrie isn't the right guy to have it with."

Jackie wished Kell and Nate could have seen Casey last night. He hadn't pushed and he hadn't taken advantage of a situation that might have played out in his favor. Instead he'd been a perfect gentleman. And kind, as well.

"I think Kell is wrong about Casey Guthrie."

Nate took a few seconds to respond. "I hope you're right. But Kell says he's got a different girl every month. Do you want to be Miss October?"

"I'm not sure who I want to be right now. But I can tell you a few things in Casey's favor. He isn't moody, he has no trouble holding down a job and he has a firm grip on reality."

Again Nate was quiet for a moment. When he spoke this time, his tone was more conciliatory. "Sometimes I forget how much you went through. What hell it must have been."

"I'm okay now. I don't want you to feel sorry for me anymore. I want to forget. To move forward. I have fun when I'm with Casey."

Actually she didn't know why she was arguing with Nate. For the most part she agreed with him. Casey might be fun, but he wasn't the right guy for her.

"Okay, okay," Nate said. "I'll back off. And I'll tell Kell to call off the P.I. we hired."

"What?"

"Just kidding. You think we're that paranoid? Besides, if we really thought you were in trouble, we'd follow the guy ourselves, not hire someone else to do it."

"Why don't I find that reassuring?"

Nate laughed. "Relax. Enjoy yourself. I'll report back to Kell that everything is fine. You have the situation under perfect control."

"Thanks, Nate." She hung up the phone with a smile.

Perfect control? Hardly. But she was working on it. She went to the living room and gazed at the wedding photograph of her and Andrew one last time. Then she wrapped it in tissue paper and took it down to storage.

CHAPTER NINE

"WANT TO SIT on the rooftop patio?" Casey asked. On the drive over he'd told Jackie about Abigail's phone call. But now that they were out on something that could reasonably be considered a real date, he wanted to forget all that for a while.

The Courage Bay Bar and Grill was one of his favorite hangouts. Usually he and his buddies preferred the bar on the main level, or played pool in the adjacent function room. But neither seemed right for his lunch with Jackie.

"Good idea. It's a beautiful day to sit and enjoy the view."

Obviously familiar with the restaurant, Jackie knew exactly where to turn to find the stairs leading up to the patio. Of course, the medical staff at the hospital hung out here, too. He'd dated a couple of nurses, a lab tech and even a doctor for a while, all of whom he'd met in this very establishment.

Gina Goodman, daughter of the owners, seated them at a table for two in a private corner. She was an attractive woman, Casey's age or a little older. Though she usually worked up here on the terrace, she filled in now and then at the bar. He'd flirted with her on more than one occasion, but they'd never gone out.

"I saw the pair of you on TV the other day." Gina poured them each a glass of ice water.

"You and the rest of Courage Bay," Casey said.

"How's the baby? I hear they finally tracked down her parents. They must have been so worried."

The case of the unidentified baby had been closely chronicled in the *Sentinel*. A big deal had been made about Haley being the granddaughter of a former mayor. So far not a whisper of anything suspicious had been associated with the story. Just another human interest feature that had begun as a tragedy—with the death of the baby-sitter—then ended on a happy and satisfying note as Haley was returned to her parents.

"The baby's fine," Casey assured Gina. "She's recovering well and she's home, safe and sound."

"Good." Gina passed them menus. "Hope you enjoy your lunch." She paused for a moment, as if considering something, then finally stepped forward and spoke quietly to Casey. "Now, you behave yourself, you hear? Jackie's not like the other girls you date."

Casey opened his mouth, not sure if he should defend himself or tell the woman to mind her own business, but Gina disappeared before he had a chance to do either. Annoyed, he glanced across the table at Jackie and saw her smiling and shaking her head.

"People keep warning me about you."

"If only they knew. I'm the one who should be warned."

"What do you mean?"

Casey bit back the impulse to make a joke, maybe something about pretty brunettes in red convertibles being irresistible to him. But Jackie appealed on a much deeper level and he wanted to be honest about that. "My life hasn't been the same since the day we met. I don't think it ever will be the same."

"That sounds…scary."

"A little. But exciting, too." He touched her hand, thinking how strange it was to feel so crazy about a woman he hadn't even kissed, not properly anyway.

The urge to do so was becoming very hard to resist. Jackie had a lovely mouth, soft lips that usually gleamed with something pink and smelled a bit like peaches. He yearned to taste that gloss, to taste the sweetness of her mouth, and wondered how long she would make him wait.

Gina returned and they placed their orders. Salad for Jackie and grilled shrimp for Casey. They covered normal getting-to-know-you topics—their jobs, places they'd traveled, things they liked to do.

Turned out they shared an affinity for adventure sports. Jackie was an experienced backcountry skier and wanted to try heli-skiing one day.

"I know this place in Kicking Horse Pass in British Columbia that's absolutely amazing," he told her. "Feels like another world." In the past, Casey's ski trips had been all-male events. But he felt excited by the idea of sharing that part of his life with Jackie.

They had barely finished eating when Casey's cell phone vibrated. After a few minutes he checked the display.

"That was my brother. Do you mind if I call him back?"

"Not at all." Jackie seemed as eager as he was to find out what Adam had to say, so he paid the bill and they left the restaurant. On the street, leaning against the side of his car with Jackie, he dialed his brother's work number.

"Adam? What's up?"

"Thought you should know we just had a report of a missing female, approximate age and description of the woman who was killed in that traffic accident."

"Finally." He'd wondered how long it would take before someone missed her.

"Yeah. This woman—name's Theresa Thatcher—became concerned when her sister, Rosie, didn't show up for their regular lunch date. She's on her way to the hospital right now to make the ID."

So the woman who'd died in the crash was named Rosie. Not Susan Smith.

"Do you know anything about this Theresa Thatcher?" Casey wondered if Rosie's sister could have been a part of the kidnapping scheme.

"Seems like a respectable young woman. In her mid-twenties, unmarried, teaches at the Orange Grove Nursery School. Claims to have been very close to her sister."

"Okay, good. Let me know if the ID is confirmed." He turned off the phone. Jackie waited, impatiently tapping her fingers against the side of his car.

"Well? Do they have a name?"

Casey filled her in on what Adam had told him. "It'll be a while before we know for sure, but Adam seems pretty confident we've found the right woman."

"Poor Theresa Thatcher. She has an awful shock in store for her. Not only will she have to deal with her sister's death, but also the possibility that she was involved in illegal activities." Jackie thought for a moment. "Do you think it's possible she knew about the kidnapping?"

"Exactly what I'm wondering. I'd love to talk to her. Maybe if we left for the hospital right now…" He glanced at his watch.

"No matter what she knows, she's just had a terrible shock. We could tell her we were the first to find her sister and at least reassure her that Rosie didn't suffer."

"That's a good idea," he said, impressed by Jackie's astuteness and sensitivity.

JACKIE AND CASEY SAT ON the bench in front of the hospital for twenty minutes before they saw a woman emerge who seemed like she might be Theresa Thatcher. She was walking alone, a little stooped, her expression bleak.

Her hair was dark, not blond like her sister's, but her features were obviously similar enough that

Casey—who'd had one awful glimpse of Rosie's face the day of the accident—was pretty sure they had the right woman.

"That's her," he whispered to Jackie.

Theresa was dressed warmly for the sunny day— brown trousers and a sweater with long sleeves that reached to her fingertips.

That she was alone tugged at Jackie's heart. Did Theresa have no one in her life to share this tragic task with? No family member or a close friend?

"Theresa Thatcher?" It was Casey who spoke first.

The woman stopped at the sound of her name. She straightened and a frown creased her smooth forehead as she spotted them. "Yes?"

"I'm Officer Casey Guthrie. And this is Jackie Kellison. We were the first people on the scene at the collision. It *was* your sister who died...?"

Theresa glanced back at the hospital, then released a heavy sigh. "Yes. It was Rosie, my baby sister."

Jackie felt Casey squeeze her fingers. She hadn't realized they were holding hands. When had that happened?

It didn't matter. What did matter was that the dead woman now had a name, and with that name, a personality, a life.

"Rosie—what a lovely name," Jackie said.

Theresa acknowledged the compliment with a sad smile. "It suited her. She had a gift for seeing the bright side of things."

An Important Message from the Editors

Dear Reader,

*Because you've chosen to read one of our fine romance novels, we'd like to say "thank you!" And, as a **special** way to thank you, we've selected <u>two more</u> of the books you love so well **plus** an exciting Mystery Gift to send you — absolutely <u>FREE</u>!*

Please enjoy them with our compliments...

Pam Powers

Lift here

How to validate your Editor's
"Thank You"
FREE GIFT

1. Peel off gift seal from front cover. Place it in space provided at right. This automatically entitles you to receive 2 FREE BOOKS and a fabulous mystery gift.

2. Send back this card and you'll get 2 brand-new *Romance* novels. These books have a cover price of $5.99 or more each in the U.S. and $6.99 or more each in Canada, but they are yours to keep absolutely free.

3. There's no catch. You're under no obligation to buy anything. We charge nothing—ZERO—for your first shipment. And you don't have to make any minimum number of purchases—not even one!

4. The fact is, thousands of readers enjoy receiving their books by mail from The Reader Service. They enjoy the convenience of home delivery...they like getting the best new novels at discount prices BEFORE they're available in stores... and they love their Heart to Heart subscriber newsletter featuring author news, horoscopes, recipes, book reviews and much more!

5. We hope that after receiving your free books you'll want to remain a subscriber. But the choice is yours— to continue or cancel, any time at all! So why not take us up on our invitation, with no risk of any kind. You'll be glad you did!

GET A *Free* MYSTERY GIFT...

SURPRISE MYSTERY GIFT COULD BE YOURS **FREE** AS A SPECIAL "THANK YOU" FROM THE EDITORS

The Editor's "Thank You" Free Gifts Include:

- *Two BRAND-NEW Romance novels!*
- *An exciting mystery gift!*

Yes!

I have placed my Editor's "Thank You" seal in the space provided above. Please send me 2 free books and a fabulous mystery gift. I understand I am under no obligation to purchase any books, as explained on the back and on the opposite page.

PLACE
FREE GIFT
SEAL
HERE

393 MDL DVFG   193 MDL DVFF

FIRST NAME	LAST NAME

ADDRESS

APT.#	CITY

STATE/PROV.	ZIP/POSTAL CODE

(PR-R-04)

Thank You!

Offer limited to one per household and not valid to current MIRA, The Best of The Best, Romance or Suspense subscribers. All orders subject to approval. Credit or debit balances in a customer's account(s) may be offset by any other outstanding balance owed by or to the customer.

▼ DETACH AND MAIL CARD TODAY! ▽

© 2003 HARLEQUIN ENTERPRISES LTD.
® and ™ are trademarks owned by Harlequin Enterprises Ltd.

The Reader Service — Here's How It Works:

BUSINESS REPLY MAIL
FIRST-CLASS MAIL   PERMIT NO. 717-003   BUFFALO, NY

POSTAGE WILL BE PAID BY ADDRESSEE

THE READER SERVICE
3010 WALDEN AVE
PO BOX 1341
BUFFALO NY 14240-8571

NO POSTAGE
NECESSARY
IF MAILED
IN THE
UNITED STATES

Seeing past Theresa's dejected air and her unflattering clothes, Jackie realized the woman had the makings of true beauty. Her skin was flawless, and she had striking facial features.

"Do you have other sisters? Brothers?"

Theresa shook her head. As her shoulders slumped again, her face became lost behind a cloud of thick hair. Jackie slipped an arm around her.

"I'm so sorry. Casey and I wanted to tell you that Rosie didn't suffer. The end was quick."

It had been brutal, too, but Theresa would have seen that when she examined the body.

"I still can't believe..." Theresa paused to use a tissue that had been scrunched in one of her hands. "When Rosie didn't show for lunch, I thought maybe her boyfriend managed to sneak away for a couple of days to take her on a holiday. It's happened before and she usually forgets to phone me." Theresa seemed to be talking more to herself than to Jackie or Casey.

"What made you call the police?" Casey asked.

"I'd seen the story in the paper about the woman killed in the accident. The age and description fit Rosie to a tee. But since Rosie drove a VW Rabbit, not a Taurus, I didn't think it could be her. Still, when I had no word from her, I decided to call to be sure. I can hardly accept that it's true."

Theresa raised her head, her eyes pleading for someone to tell her that this was all a dreadful mistake. "Why wasn't she driving her own car? And why did she have that kid in the back seat? Rosie didn't like kids much. She was always saying she could never work in a nursery school like me."

Jackie glanced at Casey. Another chink in the Voltzes' cover-up story. "As far as you knew, your sister hadn't taken on any new baby-sitting jobs?"

"No." Theresa reconsidered. "Well, I suppose it's *possible*. Actually, she must have. I can't think of any other reason for that baby to have been in her car. The police said she must have stolen it, but I can't believe that. Rosie wouldn't know *how* to steal a car."

Theresa looked at the keys she was holding as if she'd never seen them before. Her hands were shaking.

"You shouldn't drive," Jackie said gently. "Do you have any family or friends we could call?"

The woman seemed about to say something, then changed her mind and shook her head. "It was just Rosie and me."

"Where's your car?" Casey asked.

She pointed to a black Accord in the parking lot.

"It should be fine there for a while. If you want, we could give you a lift home." Casey's eyebrows went up as he looked in Jackie's direction. "If Jackie doesn't mind squeezing into the back of my car."

It *would* be tight in the rear seat of Casey's Saab, but of course Jackie didn't mind. She took Theresa's hand as they walked to the spot where he'd parked, chatting about insignificant things. The weather. A peculiar vanity license plate. The silly impracticality of two-seater convertibles with little more than a bench for luggage in the back.

They were arranging themselves in the Saab,

Casey trying not to laugh as Jackie struggled to come up with an elegant way of gaining entry to the back seat, when someone called out from behind them.

"Excuse me! Could I ask a few questions, please?"

It was the TV reporter from KSEA, waving his arms and running in their direction. Jackie recalled his name now, Don Hardrick.

"Oh, please!" Theresa put up her arm to block her face from view. "Don't let him see me!"

The reporter had no cameraman to slow him down. He dashed up behind the car, making it impossible for Casey to reverse out of the parking spot.

"Was that your sister who was killed in the accident?"

Theresa continued to hide behind the cover of her arms.

"For heaven's sake!" Jackie glared at the intruder. "Can't you give the woman a break?"

Hardrick focused on her. "What about you? You're the nurse who found the baby, right? Jackie, can you confirm the identity of the woman who died in the accident for our viewers?" He held out a small microphone.

"Please step out of the way." Casey's voice was calm but firm. "You're blocking my car."

The reporter was undeterred. "Can you tell us her name? How long had she been baby-sitting for the Voltz family?"

"Ignore him," Jackie advised Theresa as Casey responded with a brusque, "No comment."

Finally, Hardrick gave up with a frown and a shake of his head. As soon as he had the room, Casey shot out of the parking space and made for the nearest exit.

THEY'D NO SOONER LEFT the hospital parking lot than Theresa asked Casey to find a public washroom. "I'm afraid I'm going to be sick."

After making sure the reporter wasn't on his tail, Casey pulled into the gas station across the street. "I'll fill up while you use the facilities."

"Would you like some help?" Jackie offered.

Already out of the car, Theresa shook her head. "No thanks."

Ten minutes later Casey had checked the oil and filled the tank with gas, while Jackie cleaned the windshield. She followed him into the store to grab some coffee.

The woman behind the counter recognized Casey and gave him a bright smile as she took his credit card.

"How are things, Casey? The Mighty Ducks are playing in town this week. I think I could score some tickets from my boss if you'd like to see another game. We had fun the last time, didn't we?"

"We had a great time, Deb," Casey said, sounding like he meant it. "The problem is my week is looking pretty busy." He moved over to make room for Jackie to set the two coffee cups on the counter.

Debbie's gaze traveled from the coffee cups, up Jackie's arm to her face, then back to Casey. Her smile slipped several notches. "Should I add these to your bill?" she asked, tipping her head at the drinks.

"Please."

Jackie felt sorry for the woman as she and Casey left the building.

"Did the two of you date long?" she asked, unable to keep a little chill from her voice.

"We went to a game together. I had tickets and I knew she was a huge fan. Don't worry, I didn't break her heart."

Casey smiled so winningly, she could almost believe it was true. And maybe it was—from Casey's perspective. Jackie suspected that the pretty woman behind the counter took the whole affair a lot more seriously than Casey did.

"So how many old girlfriends do you have?" she asked as they leaned against his car, sipping their coffee and waiting for Theresa.

"Definitely under a hundred." He winked. "Anyway, Deb doesn't count. I never even kissed her. I tell you, we were just buddies taking in a little hockey."

She believed him, not that it really mattered. Casey was the sort of guy who broke hearts without even trying, and that was what made him truly dangerous. She had no claim on Casey Guthrie, yet when that clerk had turned her fawning eyes on him, Jackie had felt like slapping her in the face.

The impulse was troublesome, to say the least. She had no business caring if Casey flirted with other women.

"You're scowling," Casey said.

He was looking at her coffee cup. She noticed it was stained pink from her lip gloss.

"I was thinking about Theresa," she lied. She *should* have been thinking about Theresa. What was she doing, fussing about that insignificant exchange between Casey and the gas clerk, when Rosie's sister was in the washroom, throwing up in her distress.

"I wonder if she had any idea what her sister was up to on the day of the accident," Jackie said.

"I would guess not. Theresa seemed completely baffled about why Rosie would have a baby in the car with her. Though she didn't completely discount the possibility that Rosie could have been hired as a baby-sitter."

"If Theresa was Rosie's partner in this caper, she'd have to do that, wouldn't she? She wouldn't want anyone looking too deeply into why Rosie had Haley Voltz in her car."

Casey trained his gaze on the door to the women's washroom. Still closed. "True. But if Theresa was lying, she's damn good at it."

"I wonder about that boyfriend of Rosie's she mentioned. Why didn't he report her missing?"

"If he's the kidnapping partner we're looking for," Casey speculated, "he'd have very good reasons for keeping out of sight."

THERESA EMERGED from the washroom quiet and very pale. She turned down Jackie's offer to buy her a coffee.

"I'd just like to go home, thanks."

She gave Casey her address, but halfway there, changed her mind.

"Would you mind driving by Rosie's place first? It's only about six blocks out of the way."

Casey hesitated. "Are you sure you're ready to go there?"

"Rosie has some photographs on her fridge that I want. It'll just take me a moment to run and get them."

She recited an address to an apartment in the low-income district of Victoria Park, and Casey made a U-turn at the next intersection. Five minutes later they were in front of Rosie's apartment building. Casey parked across the street, by a dilapidated duplex.

At first Theresa didn't get out of the car. She gazed at the apartment building with sad longing. Probably she was thinking of the last time she'd seen her sister. Remembering how painful it was, returning to her house after Andrew's death, Jackie rested a hand on Theresa's arm.

"It's hard, isn't it?"

Theresa nodded. "I really loved my sister."

Of course she had loved her sister. Jackie wondered why she would think the words needed to be said. Before she could consider it any further, Theresa seemed to gather her mental and physical resources and climbed out of the car, heading for the main door to the apartment. Casey looked a little uncomfortable.

"What's wrong?" Jackie asked him.

"If Rosie kidnapped Haley, and kept her here,

then her apartment is a crime scene. Important evidence could be compromised by Theresa's visit."

"What can we do?"

"Not much, since we have no warrant. But maybe we could keep an eye on Theresa." As he spoke, he climbed out of the car.

"Right." Jackie vaulted out of the back seat and jogged along with him to the building.

Theresa, who had a set of her sister's keys, was opening the front door. She seemed surprised to see them. "I'll only be a second."

Casey didn't say anything about a crime scene to her, of course. Instead he mumbled something about how she shouldn't have to deal with all the memories on her own.

Theresa looked inclined to argue, but in the end she nodded. They entered the building together and checked out the small lobby. The elevator was out of order, so they took the stairs to the second floor.

"Wait for me here," Theresa said, slipping inside, then closing the door gently, but not all the way. Undeterred, Casey tapped the door with his toe, causing it to swing slowly inward so they could see what was going on.

The front entrance opened on a hall that led to a messy but colorful kitchen. The distinctive odor of old diapers wafted out, and Jackie's attention was drawn to a pail filled with disposables by the kitchen counter. Also in clear view were several used baby bottles and a container of powdered infant formula.

Clearly, Rosie had kept the baby here, and for more than a few hours of baby-sitting.

"Would the police consider this evidence of kidnapping?" Jackie asked, keeping her voice low so Theresa wouldn't hear.

"I doubt it," Casey said. "But I sure do."

CHAPTER TEN

"DID YOU GET YOUR PHOTOS?" Casey asked. He didn't
want Theresa messing around in Rosie's apartment
any more than necessary. If he could have kept her
out entirely, he would have. But Theresa had a key,
and until, and if, this place was cordoned off as a
crime scene, she had every right to be here.

Theresa glanced over her shoulder at him. "Just
a second."

She disappeared into a back room for a few moments, then returned to the kitchen. As she pulled
photos from the magnets that held them to the front
of the refrigerator, Casey scanned as much of the
apartment as he could.

Rosie had not been much of a housekeeper and
the place was a mess, but the nature of the mess
made him guess she'd last left this room in a hurry.
A glass of juice on the counter was still half full. A
couple of coats lay tossed on the floor by the door
as if she had been unable to decide what to wear.

Or maybe she'd been searching the pockets for
something. Her keys?

No, because there on the floor was a chain with

two keys. One obviously for the apartment, the second a fat, long Volkswagen key.

His attention shifted back to the jackets. Something seemed odd…

Cautiously he stepped over the threshold and lifted one sleeve with the tips of his fingers. Peering under, he spied…a frying pan?

He lifted the coat higher.

Theresa looked at him. "My sister was a bit of a slob. I really should clean this place." She tapped the pail of dirty diapers with the tip of her shoe. "The smell is terrible."

"Later," Casey suggested quickly. "You've had enough to deal with today."

"I guess you're right."

But she left with obvious reluctance.

"I'd love to see a picture of your sister." Jackie glanced with curiosity at the photos in Theresa's hand, while Casey secured Rosie's apartment.

"This was taken last Christmas." Theresa held out a close-up of a blond, dark-eyed woman with pretty features and a shy smile.

"You said she had a boyfriend?" Casey prodded.

Theresa's smile faded. "She did, but he was no good. He was older than Rosie and from a wealthy family. He treated her like garbage. He'd demand to see her on short notice, then disappear for a week without any word. I told Rosie so many times she deserved better."

"What was his name?"

Anger flared in Theresa's dark eyes, so much like

those of her sister in the photograph. "Rosie never introduced us. She knew I disapproved of him and she did her best to keep us apart."

"Where did your sister work?"

"Rosie didn't work. She didn't need to work." Theresa glanced down at the photo again, then away. "I should go home."

"Wait a minute." Rosie had been found in a stolen vehicle. And yet he'd seen a Volkswagen key on her floor. "Did your sister park her car nearby?"

"Yes, she rented a space in the parkade in the basement."

"Would you mind if we took a look?"

"I guess." She frowned. "I still can't believe Rosie stole that car. It doesn't make *sense*."

Casey borrowed Theresa's keys again to unlock the apartment. He scooped Rosie's key chain from the floor. "That's what we've been wondering, too, Theresa. Let's check it out."

They passed the broken elevator again on their way to the basement. Not only the elevator, but the entire building had the aura of a place that wasn't working. The carpet was worn and dirty, the walls needed fresh paint.

If Rosie had been a kept woman, she hadn't been kept very well.

At the bottom of the stairs, Casey held the heavy fire door open for Jackie and Theresa. They entered the underground parking lot, where spaces were tight and the lighting was poor. The slap of their footsteps on pavement echoed against the concrete walls.

"This was her stall." Theresa stopped in front of an older model Volkswagen Rabbit. The bright green car was dusty, but otherwise in good condition.

Except all four tires had been slashed.

"Well, now we know why Rosie stole the Taurus," Jackie said.

BY THE TIME they'd delivered Theresa Thatcher to her own apartment, the bereaved woman's shock had dissipated into weariness. Jackie insisted on seeing her tucked under a comforter on the sofa, since Theresa refused to go to bed. She heated a mug of instant soup and placed a plate of crackers and cheese nearby.

As she ministered to Theresa's needs as best she could, Casey prowled the place, touching nothing, but observing closely. Jackie would be interested to hear his impressions later. For herself, she was intrigued by how different Theresa's apartment was from her sister's. It was clean and tidy, with silk pillows and several beautiful watercolors.

Unable to think of anything else she could do to help, Jackie finally had to stop fussing. "Are you sure there's no one we can call?" It didn't seem right to leave the woman alone.

"No one." Theresa's head drooped back on the cotton-covered pillow Jackie had brought out from her bedroom. Even Theresa's grief and fatigue couldn't detract from her beauty—the strong bone structure, dramatic eyes and rich coloring.

An interesting woman. Her home didn't look like the home of a nursery school teacher. And it seemed strange she had no friends or family other than her sister.

The apartment offered no clues to assuage Jackie's curiosity. There were no framed photographs or personal mementoes on display. The stark black of Theresa's refrigerator wasn't marred by so much as one magnet or child's drawing. That must be why she'd been adamant about going to Rosie's to get the pictures of her sister. Maybe they were the only ones she had.

Jackie scrawled her phone number on a piece of scrap paper from her purse. "Call me if you need anything."

"Thanks, Jackie. And, Casey, too. You've been really great. I'm sorry...I can't seem to keep my eyes open."

"That's fine—sleep will be good for you. We'll call later to make sure you're okay." Jackie followed Casey through the door, down the slick, silent elevator and out to the street. It was dark now—where had the day gone?

"Hungry?" Casey asked.

"Actually, yes."

They stopped for burgers and shakes at a place a few blocks from where Jackie lived. They didn't speak much. It was hard not to worry about Theresa, alone with her grief in that too silent apartment. Or to wonder about Rosie and the choices she'd made.

"I have a feeling Rosie's boyfriend is the key to this puzzle." Jackie scrunched up the paper wrappings from her veggie burger.

"Strange that Theresa didn't know his name."

"Rosie knew her sister didn't approve of their relationship."

"Still, if the sisters were close, you'd think his name would have been mentioned at least once."

"What did you think of Theresa's apartment?"

"Impersonal," was his verdict. "At least Rosie's, dump that it was, had some personality to it. Ready to go?"

They drove to Jackie's condo and Casey walked her to her door as he'd done several times already. Jackie stopped puzzling over Theresa's and Rosie's lives and began focusing on her own.

Here was this sexy, good-looking cop standing on her doorstep. Most of the time she felt so comfortable with him. Moments like this, though, drove her anxiety—and her anticipation—skyward.

Would he kiss her good-night this time? *Really* kiss her, the way she could tell he'd wanted to do the other night when she'd frozen up on him.

Did she want him to?

She unlocked her door and looked at him hesitantly.

"You're tired," he said. She thought she was off the hook, until he added, "I think you need a neck massage."

She paused, knowing she would be sending him a message with her answer. "Are you volunteering?"

"Hell, yeah." He touched his hand to the side of her face.

She swallowed. Such a simple thing, a man placing his fingers on her cheek, and yet the effect was overwhelming.

"Come in, Casey. I think we need to talk."

She went inside herself, dropping her purse and keys near the door. Casey took care of locking the door. She heard the sound of the dead bolt turning as she headed for the kitchen to put on the coffeepot. The last time she'd gone through this ritual, neither one of them had had a drop. She wondered why she bothered, and suspected it was because she felt she needed an excuse for having a man in her apartment in the evening.

Suddenly her ploy seemed silly. Why was she playing these games?

She replaced the lid on her coffee canister, then went to find Casey. He was standing by the table where he'd seen her wedding photograph last time.

"It's gone?"

"I decided it was time to put it away."

His gaze locked on her and she could tell he understood the ramifications of that one small action. Her heart was pounding so loudly now, she wondered if he could hear that, too. Could he guess the real reason she had invited him into her apartment? It seemed important, suddenly, for her to be as honest as possible with him.

"I'm not going to make coffee." She didn't want to end up being Miss October, but neither did she want to let go of the feeling that she was truly alive again.

"No coffee. I can cope with that." Watching her carefully, he moved toward her. "Did you want that massage I promised you?"

"Not really."

He was within touching distance now and, as he held out an arm, he asked, "Are you ready for this, Jackie?"

"Actually no. That's what I wanted to talk about. There are things you don't know about me. Important things." He wouldn't *want* to kiss her if he knew. Men like Casey did everything they could to avoid complications.

"I know you have secrets, Jackie. Something from your past." He looped his arms around her waist, bringing his face achingly close to hers.

"Before we go any further, you should know—"

"There's nothing I need to know," he contradicted her. Then, as if to prove it, he kissed her. For a long time his mouth was tender and seeking, then gradually his kisses heated with passion.

Jackie felt something inside her let go, some muscle that she'd been holding tight for at least two years, maybe longer. Her heart was finally, finally breaking free.

Casey's technique was flawless. Even better, though, was the emotion she could see in his eyes and feel in his touch.

This was not just another kiss. She was not just another pretty girl.

"Jackie, you're amazing. Do you know that?"

He made her feel amazing. "Casey?"

"Shh, Jackie. Don't talk. Not yet." His mouth opened over hers again and she lost herself to the most incredible kiss yet.

Gradually he pulled back. "Regrets?" he asked.

Briefly, Andrew's face came to mind, and with it an echo of the pain and recriminations.

"No regrets," she said, but she knew it wasn't true. She would always have regrets.

She leaned her face against his chest and heard his pounding desire in her ear. He stroked her back with gentling hands.

She didn't know how he had been able to tell that she'd gone as far as she could tonight. But he had. She could feel his muscles tensing with the effort of reining himself in.

"I'm sorry," she whispered.

"Tell me what's bothering you," he said softly.

"I will," she promised. But not tonight.

A big part of Jackie wanted Casey to spend the night, but she knew she wasn't ready. When it happened, making love with him was going to be spectacular. But much as waiting for that first kiss had made the experience all the more breathtaking, so would waiting to make love.

All this Jackie knew with certainty, yet it was still difficult to say good-night to Casey, to watch him walk out her apartment door and see him blow one final kiss in her direction.

Her biggest consolation was the knowledge that they'd be having breakfast together the next morning. Casey had promised to bring lattes and muffins right to her door.

Breakfast. Now what would Nate say about that?

WAKING EARLY the next morning, Jackie knew that she had gone beyond the point of being influenced by her brothers' opinions of Casey. They knew of his reputation, but they didn't really know him. Not the way she did.

Jackie was aware that her feelings might be delusional. Women all over the world were always trying to convince themselves that the man they wanted was somehow better than he seemed.

Rosie Thatcher was the perfect example. She'd dated a man her sister hadn't approved of. A man who, from Theresa's accounts, had not treated her with respect. Why did women do that? Because they were so afraid of being alone? Because the poor treatment was all they felt they deserved? Now Rosie was dead, and she'd never find true love.

Is that what you think you've found with Casey, then? True love?

Hardly, her cynical side scoffed. And yet...

When Casey buzzed the outside security door at exactly eight-thirty, Jackie's heart leaped with a happiness she hadn't experienced in years. She eagerly pressed the button to unlock the main security door, then went to greet him at the entrance.

"Jackie."

Every time he showed up at her door, it felt like a small miracle to her.

He kissed her good morning. And despite having both hands full of their breakfast, plus the newspaper, he made sweet work of it, too.

"Well, good morning." She felt as decadent and sexy as if she'd woken up in bed with him. *Be careful, Jackie. This feels good, but don't be too reckless.*

She placed the muffins on the counter, next to the tray of lattes and the rolled up paper. "Did you buy anything with chocolate chips?" She peered inside the bag of muffins.

"I did."

"Well, I have dibs on that one."

His smile was indulgent. "Lucky for you I bought two."

They ate leisurely on the floor of her living room, taking turns reading the newspaper to each other. Rosie Thatcher's identification had earned a short article on the second page of the city section. Once finished with that, Casey flipped to the comics and made Jackie laugh with his silly dramatizations.

Jackie sipped her creamy latte and wondered at how quickly her life had gone from the routine to the tragic to the sublime.

Then Casey said, "Look what I've got." He pulled a photograph from his pocket and passed it to her.

The picture was of Rosie and Theresa. The two sisters had their arms wrapped around each other, and their heads—one blond, the other dark—tipped to touch at the crown.

"What is this? Where did you get it?"

"Theresa dropped it in my car. I found it this morning."

"We should take it back to her. I got the impression she doesn't have many photos of her sister."

"We'll do that. But first, I thought we might try a little experiment."

She reached over to wipe a smudge of chocolate chip from the corner of his mouth. "What did you have in mind?"

"I can't believe a woman like Rosie, with no prior convictions, would decide to kidnap a child on a random basis. There has to be an association between Rosie and the Voltz family."

"That makes sense. But if there was some sort of relationship, do you think any of the Voltzes will admit it?"

"Probably not voluntarily. But I'd like to gauge their reactions when I show them this picture. Bill Voltz, at least, should remember whether this is the woman who posed as Susan Smith."

CHAPTER ELEVEN

Sɪɴᴄᴇ Bɪʟʟ ᴡᴏᴜʟᴅ ʙᴇ at work, Casey and Jackie decided to try the older Voltz couple first. Employees from a gardening service were busy working on the mansion grounds when they arrived. A young man in dark green trousers with a matching shirt was trimming the already perfect lawn with a riding mower while his identically dressed cohort deadheaded the chrysanthemum border at the front of the house.

With Theresa's photograph tucked safely into a manila envelope under his arm, Casey traversed the stone walk, Jackie by his side. She was game for anything, Casey thought, and that was one of the qualities he found most appealing about her.

She didn't hold back. She'd been unstoppable at the emergency scene and tenacious in her desire to protect Haley. After experiencing what it was like to kiss her, Casey suspected she'd be just as uninhibited in the bedroom. Time would tell on that score— he hoped.

If she had been any other woman, they'd have slept together at least once by now. But for Jackie, he was willing to wait. By now he was sure her issues had to do with her deceased husband, but Andrew had been gone for two years. Wasn't that long enough to have moved on? Surely he wasn't the first guy Jackie had dated in all that time.

"It's already ten." Jackie stopped as they reached the front door. She attempted to peer past the colorful stained-glass inlay. "Maybe no one will be home."

He put a thumb on the front door buzzer and held it for a second. From inside, he heard the chime announcing their arrival.

Someone was there, all right. Wallace Voltz tore the door open with enough gusto to threaten the hinges.

When he recognized them, his overt anger was replaced with watchful caution.

"I thought you were more journalists. They've been hounding us ever since that woman was identified yesterday."

"Rosie Thatcher," Casey said deliberately.

Wallace avoided his gaze. "I guess that's right."

"You still don't remember her, sir?"

"No reason why I should. My son, Bill, is the one who hired her."

"Right." Casey eyed him carefully. Wallace was smooth, but his body language revealed more than he realized. He was worried, and not just about pesky journalists.

"I wonder if we could come in for a moment. I'd like your opinion on something." Casey held up the envelope. "Mrs. Voltz, too, if she's home."

"You've caught me at a bad time."

"We could return in an hour."

The older man sighed. "Might as well get this over with. But you'll have to do without Abigail. She's previously engaged."

They were ushered to a study with enough book-filled shelves to be considered a small library. Wallace offered coffee, then gave them an update on Haley, who was apparently recovering well from her surgery.

Casey was glad to hear it, but he had the impression Wallace was marking the minutes before he could politely show them the door. While they talked, he kept glancing toward the hall, a tic in his left eye revealing anxiety.

Casey suspected he was afraid his wife might make an unexpected appearance and spill more of the family secrets. Probably Abigail wasn't "otherwise engaged" this morning, at all.

After opening the envelope, Casey handed Wallace the photograph.

"What's this?" He held the picture at arm's length, squinting slightly.

"That's the woman who died in the car accident. Rosie Thatcher."

"Oh, my Lord." Wallace stared again at the photograph. "Who's that other woman? The one on the left?"

"The one on the left *is* Rosie Thatcher," Jackie explained. "She died in the car crash. The other woman is her sister, Theresa."

Casey glanced at Jackie, then back at Wallace. "Now that you see the picture, do you remember ever meeting Rosie?"

"Of course not," Wallace said, speaking much too quickly and vehemently to be believed. He dragged his gaze away from the photo. "Would you mind if I kept this? I'd like to show Abigail when she comes home."

"I'm afraid I can't. It doesn't belong to me." Casey held out his hand and reluctantly Wallace dropped the photograph into his palm.

Casey decided to press a little harder. "Are you standing by your story that Haley *wasn't* kidnapped?"

Anger tightened the lines at the corners of Wallace's mouth. "I've already explained about that. My wife was distraught. We all were."

"If you're covering up a kidnapping, you could be placing children at risk, Mr. Voltz. Maybe even Haley."

"Haley couldn't be safer. We have a nurse on the premises twenty-four hours a day, and her parents are extremely vigilant, let me assure you." Wallace reverted to the formal bearing with which he'd answered the door. "Even if Haley had been kidnapped, her abductor is now dead." He glanced at the photo Casey still held in his hand. "Rosie Thatcher can't hurt my granddaughter now."

"Not Rosie, no," Casey agreed, returning the picture to the envelope. "But what if Rosie was working with an accomplice? Have you thought of that possibility?"

Wallace's posture became even stiffer. "Haley is home where she belongs. There's no point to any of these questions, Officer Guthrie."

"I'm not here in an official capacity."

"Good. Because we have better things to do with our tax dollars than beat dead horses." He glanced pointedly at Jackie, "Like funding our hospitals."

Was that a threat? Casey wondered. No more questions about the kidnapping or the Voltzes' annual contribution to the hospital might be in jeopardy?

But Wallace didn't give them the opportunity to make further inquiries. Deftly he led them to the front entrance, talking all the while, giving them no chance to break into the conversation.

At the door, he thanked them again for rescuing Haley. For their continued concern.

"But no need to worry anymore," he finished. They were both on the landing now, propelled by the sheer force of Wallace Voltz's personality. "Haley is fine. The family will keep a close eye on her, you can be sure of that."

With a final goodbye, the door was closed firmly in their faces.

CASEY STEPPED OVER the litter of dead chrysanthemum blossoms that the gardeners hadn't yet swept from the stone pathway.

"So what was that about?" Jackie threw a final look back at the door, her expression thoughtful.

"Wallace recognized Rosie."

"More than that, Casey. Did you see his face when

he saw the picture? That woman meant something to him. The way he pretended to mix up the sisters—I think he was trying to recover from his shock."

"Any thoughts on what, exactly, Rosie might have meant to Wallace Voltz?"

Jackie paused to weigh her words carefully. "It's a long shot, but do you think he could have been Rosie's boyfriend? Theresa said her sister was seeing someone older and wealthy. Someone who would disappear for a week at a time—maybe because he was married?"

Casey looked at her appreciatively. "Bingo."

HIS WHOLE WORLD was falling apart. And there seemed to be nothing he could do to stop it.

Wallace Voltz crumpled the newspaper article he'd been reading before Jackie Kellison and Casey Guthrie showed up. It wasn't front-page news anymore, but there'd been a story in the *Sentinel* confirming that the dead woman had been identified as Rosie Thatcher. He knew it was unrealistic to think the reporters would lose all interest in the story. But he did hope to spare Abigail these worrying details. He threw the entire newspaper into the fireplace, then with a flick of his wrist, lit one of the long matches stored near the hearth and tossed that in, too.

The paper burned satisfactorily for a few minutes. Finally the entire edition was nothing but a mound of ash.

He wished he could purge the information he'd learned this morning from his mind as easily.

That damn woman. He should have known.

Wallace went to the stainless-steel carafe on his desk and poured himself another cup of coffee. Unfortunately it was much too early for Scotch. God, he could use a drink.

China cup in hand, he paced the length and breadth of the room, wondering what the hell he should do.

At his age, it was the rare man who hadn't figured out that only two things counted in this life: money and family. He had a guaranteed source of the first, but the second was a matter of deep concern these days.

His marriage had begun as a practical one and was something he had never regretted. His relationship with his son, however, was another matter. He'd tried when Bill was younger, but every venture, from father-son fishing trips to coaching Bill's Little League baseball, had met with abysmal failure.

With Haley's arrival, he'd hoped to finally have a child with whom he could connect. Whenever he held the infant in his arms, he felt his future was full of possibilities. He saw himself taking her to the park and teaching her to ride a bike and reading stories at night.

When the baby was a little older, he and Abigail intended to offer to baby-sit at every opportunity. They'd even prepared a bedroom at their house, just for her.

That was Wallace's dream. But what would happen if the family fell apart? Divorce had a way of bringing out bitterness and vindictiveness. His rights as a grandfather might not carry as much weight in the courts as he'd like.

Infidelity was a delicate endeavor, Wallace reflected. It had to be conducted with great sensitivity and discretion. And brevity was always smart, too. Otherwise, what started as a short-term indiscretion could end up tearing a man apart and destroying everything he'd worked his life to build. He had seen this vice destroy his family in the past, and he feared it was about to happen again.

For Haley's sake, he'd done his best to mitigate the damage. This little girl deserved to grow up in a stable, loving home, with a mother and father and two doting grandparents. Maybe they weren't perfect, but they were Haley's family. So far the inner circle had been protected, but Casey Guthrie had worried him today.

The officer's talk about an accomplice was all too plausible, especially now that Wallace had seen that picture of the Thatcher sisters.

If only that stupid woman could have remained unidentified. He had no doubt that probing into Rosie Thatcher's life would eventually lead to—

He poured his next cup of coffee and was pleased to see his hand was steady. He couldn't let one greedy, immoral young woman destroy his family.

And he wouldn't.

IN ORDER TO CONFIRM their theory, Casey and Jackie needed a photograph of Wallace Voltz. They decided to check the public library archives of the *Courage*

Bay Courier. Jackie found a fairly decent shot of Wallace Voltz at one of the charity functions he patronized. They took a photocopy and the result was a black-and-white picture that, although grainy, offered a pretty good likeness.

Their plan was to show the picture around to the residents of Rosie Thatcher's apartment building to see if anyone could remember seeing Voltz with Rosie.

As Jackie had said, it was a long shot, but they might get lucky.

Driving toward Rosie's Victoria Park address, Casey sensed Jackie's growing excitement.

"I always wondered what it would be like to be a detective," she said. "It's a real kick."

"Mostly it's a lot of boring legwork, interspersed with a lot of boring paperwork. That's what Adam says, anyway." But he had to admit, he liked this stuff, too.

"Doesn't Adam enjoy his job?"

"Enjoy is too mild a word. I can't imagine my brother being anything but a police detective. That guy eats, drinks and sleeps his work." Or at least he had before Faith.

"What about you? Do you love your job that much, too?"

"Maybe once I did. I've had fun on traffic patrol." He'd met more than his share of pretty women by pulling them over for speeding, then starting to chat. It didn't seem to matter whether he issued a citation or not. Many were still willing to go out with him.

But that had been a game for a young man. Casey was getting bored of it. "I can't believe ten years have gone by since I started." Ten years. Man, what had happened to the time? "It hasn't felt that long."

"I know what you mean. I've worked almost that long in the ER. I'm hooked on the adrenaline rush, though. I can't imagine settling for the routine of any other department."

Once, maybe even a few months ago, Casey would have said the same about his job. Now he wasn't so sure.

He'd scoffed when Adam had announced his decision to go for detective many years ago. As far as Casey had been concerned back then, life didn't get any finer than pulling in a paycheck for cruising around on a BMW bike in the warm California sunshine.

But what had been cool at twenty-five might be a little old by thirty-five. And if he didn't want to end up in that situation, he had to start planning his next move soon.

In a sweeping glance, Casey took in the tightly packed real estate of Victoria Park.

"Quite a contrast to Vista Drive, isn't it?" Jackie pushed her sunglasses up on her head.

They were two different worlds, all right, the opulent Jacaranda Heights mansions and these low-income apartment buildings, most without even a pretense at a front garden, only crushed rock and pavement and a few scraggly shrubs. He parked the car, turned off the motor.

"Now what?" Jackie asked.

He shrugged. "We get out of the car and start talking to people."

They made their way to the front entrance of the apartment. A woman pushed a stroller ahead of them, then stopped to struggle with the heavy security door. Casey winked at Jackie before stepping forward.

"Can I help you, ma'am?" Casey eased the door wide with one hand and helped lift the stroller up a final step with the other.

The woman didn't thank him, just looked at him suspiciously. "I haven't seen you in this building before. Who are you?"

"Officer Casey Guthrie with the Courage Bay Police Department, ma'am."

Her wary expression transformed into instant approval. "Thank you very much, Officer." She pushed the stroller safely inside, not at all concerned when Casey and Jackie followed behind her. Partway to the elevator, which was working now, she paused and turned around.

"Are you here because of that woman who died in the accident?" Without allowing enough time for him to answer, she asked another question. "I heard a rumor she was driving a stolen car. Is that true? Wait a minute…" Her eyes brightened.

"You're the cop on the motorcycle, aren't you?" For the first time she seemed to notice Jackie. "And you're the nurse. Oh, that was so romantic. So are you, like, a couple now?"

Casey looked at Jackie, not sure how she would

react. It seemed their one minute of fame had been observed—and remembered—by most of Courage Bay. To his relief, she seemed amused rather than annoyed by the woman's comments.

"We're working on the couple thing," he finally said. "And you're right, the reason we're here is because of Rosie Thatcher. Do you remember her at all?"

"Sure. She lived in the apartment next to mine."

What a stroke of luck! "Did you ever notice any boyfriends hanging around? Say, someone who might have looked like this guy?" He stood back a little so Jackie could show her the photocopied picture.

"Hmm. He's pretty old for Rosie. And I don't remember seeing him. She didn't have many visitors, except for her sister. She lived a quiet life. Kept to herself. I tried to start up a conversation a few times when we first moved in. She cut me right off."

A bell sounded and the single elevator door opened in front of them.

"I should go. Joel's going to wake up any second and want his bottle."

"Sure. Thanks for the help." Casey held the elevator door open until she and the stroller were both inside.

He and Jackie lingered in the lobby for fifteen minutes, talking to the various tenants who came and went. No one recognized the man in the photograph. Most hadn't even realized the woman in the news had actually lived in their building.

BY SIX O'CLOCK it seemed safe to assume that Bill Voltz would be home from work. Casey and Jackie drove back to his neighborhood and knocked on the door.

Bill answered, still in his suit from the office. "Didn't we agree on Friday night?" he asked.

"We have a quick question. We'll only take a minute." Casey held up the photograph of the two sisters. "Is this the woman who took Haley from you? The one who posed as Susan Smith?"

Bill looked annoyed, but more than that, worried. "I told you she was wearing a hat and sunglasses." Still, he accepted the photograph and scrutinized it.

"Could be her," he said after twenty seconds or so. He shoved the picture back at Casey, but just then Sherri-Ann came out of the kitchen.

"What's going on?"

Casey explained once again and showed her the picture. Her eyes rounded, but she didn't say a thing.

"Are both of you still standing by your statement that Haley was never kidnapped?" Jackie asked.

"Of course I am. Anyway, it doesn't matter." Bill's gaze dropped back to the photograph. "She's dead, right? I have to go. Come back tomorrow if you still want to see Haley."

"IT'S ALL VERY STRANGE, isn't it?" Jackie sat cross-legged on the floor in her living room. She had the door to the balcony open and seemed unperturbed at the way the cool breeze ruffled the smooth layers of her chocolate-brown hair.

Casey had a whole list of things he liked about this

woman. Near the top was the way she never fussed with her appearance. She didn't complain about the wind in her hair when they were driving, she didn't wear too much makeup, and she managed to dress nicely without ever being in heels that were too high for running or skirts too short for bending.

"What do you mean?" They'd ordered pizza again—it seemed they never had time for real food. Casey polished off his third slice.

"You'd think *someone* would have seen Wallace Voltz entering or leaving that apartment building at some point. That is, if we're right about him being Rosie's married lover."

"Maybe they had a different meeting place. I have difficulty picturing someone with as much money as Voltz in a dump like Rosie's."

"I suppose he'd prefer posh hotels and room service."

"Definitely more his style."

"So what went wrong with the affair, do you think? I suppose they fought about his wife."

"Then Rosie turned vindictive, posed as a baby-sitter to his son and ran off with his granddaughter. That might explain the slashed tires. Voltz realizes what she's up to and disables her vehicle. Then she outmaneuvers him by stealing a car."

"But if Wallace knew where she lived, why not call the police?"

"I'm guessing he would have done that as a last resort only. He didn't want his family to know about his affair. Maybe he thought he could talk Rosie out of her snit. Or maybe he decided giving her the money was easiest of all. Wouldn't that be ironic if Rosie was killed when she was trying to bring the baby home?"

"Ironic, Casey? Or tragic?"

"Maybe both." Casey put aside the pizza carton and the two cans of beer they'd just finished. "How's your neck? You seem to be moving a little easier today. We should have dropped in at a clinic."

"The muscles have loosened up on their own. I don't need any therapy."

He urged her closer, arranging her so that she sat in the vee of his outspread legs with her back facing him. Gently he kneaded the muscles that had been clenched tight after the accident and saw that they were indeed relaxing.

He continued massaging, though, using gentle pressure to avoid further injury. "Feel okay?"

"Heaven, Casey. Heaven."

He chuckled. "That's what all the girls say."

It was the wrong joke to make, because she immediately stiffened.

"Sorry." He nuzzled his chin against her hair. "Forget I said anything about other girls. I meant what I told you the other night, Jackie. This isn't just fun and games for me."

She considered his words for a moment. "Maybe that's how you feel now. But, Casey, it's hard for me to take you seriously when we haven't even known each other a week and I've already met two of your ex-girlfriends."

"Two?"

"Gina and Debbie."

"I'm telling you, I never dated either of them."

"Okay, maybe not those two in particular. But plenty of others, right?"

Casey sighed and his hands stilled on her shoulders. "Adam said my past would catch up to me eventually, and I guess it has."

"I'm sorry." She tried to stand. "Your love life really isn't any of my business."

He held her where she was. "I don't have any dark secrets. I've gone out with lots of women. Had two relationships that lasted more than six months but not quite a year. I'd be the first to say that commitment has never been my strong suit, but that was before I met you."

"Am I really so different from all the others?"

"Yes."

His simple answer seemed to be enough. She leaned back into him and he wrapped his arms around her waist. Her hair smelled clean and minty, her body felt warm and sexy.

"Tell me about your past, Jackie. Tell me about Andrew."

He held his breath, wondering if she would answer. And then, finally, she did.

"I met Andrew about six years ago. He was a patient in the ER. Burst appendix."

Though he couldn't see her face, she sounded as if the memory made her smile. Casey pushed aside the uncharitable prickle of jealousy. "What did he do for a living?"

Jackie tensed. "Andrew was a dabbler. While we were married, he worked for a painting contractor and a landscaping company. He was a barkeep, taught swimming, worked in a restaurant kitchen."

"Got bored easily, did he?"

She hesitated. "Actually, he got fired easily. Andrew was an excellent worker when he was in a good mood. But he'd get into a funk. At those times he seemed like a totally different person."

"That must have been hard to live with."

She didn't say anything, and he realized she didn't want to criticize her dead husband. He admired her loyalty.

"How long were you married?"

"Three years. We had some good times."

The way she said that, it was clear there'd been lots of bad times, too. In fact, Casey was left with the impression that the bad may have outweighed the good.

Was that why Jackie was so cautious with her heart now? Having had one bad experience with marriage, was she leery of falling in love again?

He began rubbing her shoulders and was surprised how much her muscles had tightened. God, she really was tense. Was this just from talking about her husband's bad employment record?

No. There was more to the story than that. And

suddenly Casey realized the one question he should have asked much earlier.

"Jackie, how did your husband die?"

CHAPTER TWELVE

JACKIE HADN'T EXPECTED her relationship with Casey to progress to this level. Now, against all odds, it seemed that it had.

Casey had stopped any pretense at massage. His hands cupped both of her shoulders and she could feel the warmth of his chest against her back.

Maybe it would be easier to tell him sitting this way—without facing him. She gathered her breath and her courage and blurted out the words.

"My husband committed suicide."

Silence fell, as she'd known it would.

Then, "Jesus, Jackie. Suicide."

She closed her eyes, gathering her strength. Saying that word was always hard, but in many ways, what came next was even harder. Casey would want to hear the details. People always did. Mostly they were too polite to ask, but a few had dared to pose the questions.

How did he kill himself?

Were you there when it happened?

Were you the one who found him?

What did you do then?

Curiosity was natural, Jackie knew, but it could be very hurtful, too. No amount of therapy would allow her to relate the events of that night with equanimity. But for a few precious people, she made the effort, because it was important that they knew and understood.

She'd told her brothers. And her therapist. And now...

"Casey, what I'm going to say isn't pretty. If you want to leave when I'm done, I won't blame you."

"You don't have to put yourself through this. Not for my sake." Casey wrapped his arms tightly around her, lowering his head next to hers.

If he only knew...

"I'm falling in love with you, Jackie Kellison."

She closed her eyes, feeling a bittersweet pleasure at his words.

"Every moment I'm with you, I sink a little deeper."

Well, he wouldn't do any more sinking when he heard what she had to say, Jackie thought. "It happened a week before Christmas, two years ago. I was coming home from my shift, it was almost midnight."

She'd talked about that night many times with her therapist and a few times with her brothers. She'd hoped repetition would dull the shock, the pain, but it hadn't. Her breath caught now, and her stomach roiled.

"I came in the side door—we lived in a house then, with a detached garage." She swallowed, picturing herself as she'd been that night, tired, her shoes in her hands so she wouldn't wake Andrew, creeping along the hallway in her stockinged feet.

"In the foyer I saw a dark shadow. My first thought was that Andrew had moved the Christmas tree out from the family room."

Casey's arms grew so tight, they felt like a band across her chest.

"But it wasn't a tree. Andrew had hung himself from the top railing of our second floor landing."

"Oh, Jackie."

Casey buried his head in the space between her shoulder and neck. She was still facing forward, staring into space. Remembering... And pulling back. There were some moments she didn't need to relive. That no one, ever, needed to hear about again.

"How could he do that?" Casey asked in a ravaged tone. "I don't just mean the suicide. Why did he do it in your house? Where you were sure—" His voice broke and he stopped to compose himself. "I'm sorry. I shouldn't have said that. Clearly he wasn't thinking straight."

"With hindsight, I've realized Andrew was bipolar. I didn't recognize it at the time, though. A friend at work once questioned me about his mood swings and I defended him wholeheartedly. I must have been in denial. What I should have done was insist he seek medical help."

"You were too close to the situation to see clearly."

"I'm a nurse. I should have known."

"You feel responsible. But you shouldn't."

"I've had two long years to review my marriage. I've approached it from every imaginable angle, blamed myself a thousand different ways."

She twisted around and finally faced Casey. In his eyes she saw so much. Pain, sadness, sympathy. And something that might be the love Casey had professed to feel.

But would he still be so enamored of her when he heard the rest?

"I didn't work for six months after it happened, Casey. I could barely function. I guess it would be fair to say I had a breakdown." She'd crumbled in the face of Andrew's suicide. She hadn't even been able to return to her house. Her brothers had packed up the place for her, saving only the most essential or treasured items.

She'd sold everything else.

Her wedding picture was one of the few mementoes of Andrew that she'd kept. She'd gone through a period of hating him, and during that time had destroyed a lot of the gifts he'd given her, as well as old photos and letters. Now that she was past all that, she felt sorry she had so little to remember him by. She was doing her best to focus on the happy times they'd shared. And she was glad she still had their wedding photo, because that had been a golden day—one of the very best.

But she was also glad she'd moved the picture to storage, because it was time, and she truly did want to move on. To find a man to marry and to be the father of her children.

Could that man be Casey?

Though he continued to defy her preconceptions of him, showing more kindness, more compassion, more patience than she would imagine him capable of, it didn't seem likely.

He saw her as a brave, strong woman. But she wasn't at all. When faced with the worst crisis of her life, she'd fallen completely to pieces. She helped strangers in the ER room on an everyday basis. But she'd failed her own husband.

Casey's hands framed her face. He kissed her on the nose, her cheeks, tenderly on the lips. She wound her arms around his back, leaning against the strength of his chest.

"I'm glad you told me," he said.

Was he really? Jackie wasn't so sure. But she wanted to be held by him so badly, she didn't say a word.

ANOTHER CORNER OF Jackie's wounded heart healed that night as Casey soothed her in his arms. They didn't make love; they both knew this wasn't the right time for that to happen. But his presence beside her was as solid a comfort as she'd ever known.

They slept on cushions on the floor, a throw from her sofa over their shoulders, until a soft peach light slid between the slats of the horizontal blinds on her south-facing window.

Casey rolled over as the light hit his eyes. Jackie felt the cold as he moved away from her. Sitting up in the pale light, she struggled to get her bearings.

She couldn't believe they'd slept on the floor all

night. Carefully she checked her neck, but the muscles didn't seem any tighter than before. She gathered the throw from the floor and placed it over Casey.

He held out a hand, which she ignored.

"Why are you up so early?" he mumbled. "Come back, Jackie."

For some reason, what had seemed so right and natural last night—lying in Casey's arms—now made her feel self-conscious and uncomfortable.

"Let me put on some coffee instead."

He propped his body up on one elbow, watching as she worked in the adjacent kitchen. "Are you avoiding me?"

Yes, she was, but she didn't tell him that. Falling asleep in his arms had been a mistake. She'd never expected him to stay all night. She'd really believed that at some point he would turn and run.

Yet he was still here.

Jackie turned on the machine, then didn't know where to focus. Not on Casey—that was too dangerous. He was looking so…nice. Mildly confused, concerned, attentive. So many people had warned her to watch out for him, and yet he was one of the best men she'd ever met.

Last night he'd said he was falling in love with her. And this morning she knew how desperately she wanted to believe him.

Only she knew that once he'd had a chance to fully process what she'd told him, his feelings would change.

"Come here, Jackie." He held out his hand again, and it was all she could do to ignore it.

"I have to take a shower first," she said, delaying the inevitable. Casey would tell her that he really liked her, had enjoyed their time together, but unfortunately…

She ducked into the bathroom.

THE BRIGHT LIGHTS in the white-tiled room, along with the cleansing spray from the shower, dispelled the last traces of intimacy that had enveloped Jackie the previous evening.

How could I have told him everything about Andrew? I haven't known the guy a week! There was only one detail she hadn't shared, but then she hadn't told anyone that. Not her therapist, not her brothers. Her husband hadn't left a note, but he'd left her a message, all right. One only she could understand.

She felt the sort of discomfort and shame that she imagined a woman would feel waking up in the morning to find that she'd made love with a man she barely knew.

Except for Jackie, sharing the details of Andrew's death was way more intimate than any sexual act.

Her cheeks burned with shame as she stepped out of the shower. If only there was some way to turn back the clock, to take back the words.

Whatever had been growing between her and Casey was spoiled now. She was so certain that he would turn and run at the first opportunity that she was surprised to see him still in her kitchen when she stepped out of the bedroom.

He was making toast and barely looked up at her. "Want some coffee?" Without waiting for her response, he poured her a cup, then passed her a plate with two pieces of buttered toast.

She sat awkwardly at one of the stools by the counter, thinking it would have been easier if he had just left. She didn't want to face him right now, her embarrassment was too acute.

He was the first to confront the problem between them.

"Did I let you down somehow last night?" he asked.

"Hardly." He'd been perfect. Too perfect.

"Then why are you looking at me as if you wouldn't trust me with a ten-dollar petty cash fund?"

He was wrong. She would trust him with anything. "Casey, you don't have to pretend nothing's changed. I know a lot of what I told you last night must have been pretty shocking."

"You don't think it changed the way I feel about you, do you?"

"Casey, I had a nervous breakdown. I was hospitalized and treated for clinical depression. And it's not like it was just for a week or two. It's only been the past couple of months that I've started to feel myself again."

"I understood the first time, Jackie. Do you think what happened to you somehow makes you unlovable? As far as I'm concerned, the way your husband treated you——"

"Please don't criticize Andrew. I won't put up with it. He was sick. It wasn't his fault."

"Well, it wasn't your fault, either."

She didn't say anything to that. Just sat there, wondering... Did he really believe what he was saying? She picked up a slice of toast and stared at the slightly burned crusts. "This is the first home-cooked meal we've eaten together."

Casey took the toast from her hand and spread a thick layer of jam on it. "Well, it's a start, I guess."

AFTER BREAKFAST, Casey and Jackie drove to his place so he could shower and change. While he dashed up to his apartment, Jackie ordered lattes from the café on the corner. They met at his car, quickly taking their usual places, their coffees secure in the cup holders.

The weather forecast came on the radio. Rain was heading toward California and would probably hit Courage Bay early this evening. Casey glanced up at the perfect blue canopy overhead and sighed for the summer that was surely at an end now.

In the seat next to him, Jackie sat, quiet and serious, as he sped along PCH toward Theresa's neighborhood. She hadn't spoken much since their conversation this morning. He guessed she needed time. And maybe another shot of caffeine wouldn't hurt, either. He took the Morningside exit off the freeway, then turned toward Theresa's apartment.

When Jackie began drumming her fingers on her disposable cup, he could tell that she felt it, too: a sense that time was running out. As soon as he parked, she was out of the car, leaving him to trail after her. They buzzed Theresa's apartment and were both disappointed when she didn't respond.

"What do we do now?" Jackie gazed anxiously up at the apartment building.

Casey counted the stories to Theresa's floor. Her windows were open.

"Do you think she's home, but too upset to answer the door?" Jackie suggested.

"Possibly. Or maybe she has something to hide." He glanced around, looking for an opportunity. When he saw an elderly woman approaching with a bag of groceries, he winked broadly at Jackie. She covered her smile with her hand as he trotted down the sidewalk to offer his help.

Using a similar technique to the one that had gained him access to Rosie's place the other day, he soon had them inside the apartment building. After seeing the older woman to her rooms, they ran down a flight to Theresa's floor. At her door they paused to listen, but couldn't hear so much as a television.

Casey tried ringing the buzzer, then rapping on the door. After about three minutes, Theresa finally responded. She seemed breathless and not happy to see them.

"I'm sorry. This isn't a good time."

"We'll only be a moment." Somehow Casey managed to edge into the apartment, forcing Theresa to step back. "We have something you dropped in the car."

Theresa's gaze flew to the envelope in his hand. "Actually, I was on my way to make funeral arrangements," she said. "I don't want to be late."

"Of course not." Jackie was all sympathy. "We should have called first. But don't worry, we'll only be a minute."

She looked at Casey expectantly, giving him the perfect opening he needed. He cracked open the envelope and fished out the photocopied picture of Wallace Voltz.

"That isn't mine." Theresa frowned.

"No, the picture you dropped is still in here." He passed her the envelope. "But I was wondering if you could tell us if you've ever seen the guy in this newspaper photograph. We have reason to believe he might have been your sister's lover."

"Oh?" Theresa's dark eyebrows rose in perfect arches. "Let me see."

As she reached out her hand, her blouse rode up her arm a little and Casey noticed a rough red patch around her wrist. Not a bruise, it looked like…rope burn.

He tried to check out her other wrist, but it was covered.

Was Theresa into kinky sexual activities? *It's always the quiet ones who surprise you.*

As she studied the clipping, he searched for any sign of recognition. In the first instant, he thought he saw her eyes widen a little, but then she shook her head and pressed her lips together tightly.

"No, I've never seen him before."

Jackie exhaled a long breath of disappointment. "Well, it was a long shot. You did tell us you'd never met her lover."

Theresa acknowledged the truth of this with a short nod.

"Do you think maybe he'll show up at the funeral?" Jackie asked.

"And risk his wife finding out about the affair?" Theresa replied in a mocking tone. "I don't think so."

So they'd been right in guessing that Rosie's boyfriend was married, Casey surmised. Theresa Thatcher might not have known exactly who her sister's lover had been, but she knew a lot about him. And clearly she blamed him for Rosie's death.

CHAPTER THIRTEEN

CASEY AND JACKIE SHARED their impressions of Theresa on the drive to Jackie's condo. Jackie had noticed the rope burn, too. What had puzzled her more, however, was Theresa's obvious desire to get rid of them quickly.

"The other day, I thought she seemed genuinely distraught about her sister's death. Now…I don't know how to put it. There was something hard about her."

It was almost noon when Casey pulled to a stop on Jackie's street. She had the door open before he'd switched off the ignition. "You don't need to walk me up."

"Wait." He put a hand on her arm and kept it there until she'd closed the door and turned back to face him.

He wondered if she had any idea how attractive she looked at that moment. The ivory of her sweater set off her creamy complexion and showcased her lovely eyes and gleaming lips. He was achingly aware of the curves under that sweater and the long wool skirt she'd teamed with it.

Casey cleared his throat. "I scared you off, didn't I? Saying I love you."

The mask she'd been wearing all morning slipped a little, exposing unhappiness and confusion. "I'm the one who put you in an uncomfortable position. We've only known each other a few days. And I exposed so much of myself. Believe me, I don't talk about Andrew to many people."

He wanted to hug her, but the don't-touch-me aura she radiated was like a physical barrier. He settled for tweaking a strand of her hair. "Of course you don't. And I'm honored that you trusted me. But I don't agree that you said too much. I think we need to talk more."

She sighed. "I couldn't. I'm so tired…"

"A walk and some fresh air might revive you."

She looked surprised by the suggestion. "Actually, I think you're right. That's exactly what I need."

"I know the perfect place, about an hour north of here. Ever been to the Golden Eagle Nature Preserve? When I was a kid, my family used to go there for hikes. Trails lead through the forest right up to an ungroomed beach."

"Sounds perfect."

He took off for the highway, with the music cranked up. Jackie liked country and he obligingly changed his radio station for her. By the time they arrived at the park, he could tell she was already much more relaxed. They left the car and he chose one of the more obscure paths.

For a long while they walked in silence. Finally he took Jackie's hand, and that was enough for him; holding her hand and having her beside him. The silence of the forest was so calming. He wondered why he didn't come out to this place more often.

"This is like going to church," Jackie said. "It's *better* than going to church. I feel so peaceful."

After about twenty minutes they reached the water's edge. The sand was coarse and littered with boulders and large pieces of driftwood. The smaller ones were scavenged quickly, something he and Adam had done when they were kids.

"Want to sit for a while?" he asked.

They picked a spot back from the sand, on a rotting tree trunk that offered a dry perch. The sky was still blue, but the wind had picked up. Out on the ocean the waves frolicked with abandon. Casey knew the storm clouds would soon be blowing in. For now, though, the day remained unseasonably warm and pleasant.

"Jackie, I can't pretend to understand all that you must have gone through with your husband's death. But I do know that you didn't deserve any of it."

She examined a piece of driftwood she'd picked up from the ground. Turned it this way and that. "Maybe I did. There were signs I should have noticed."

"You're not a clinical psychologist." He recalled that business letter he'd spotted in her kitchen the first day he'd met her. He was so glad now he hadn't pried any further.

"No, I'm not a psychologist, but I am a trained medical professional. Andrew always had mood swings, but they were worse in the months before—" She sighed. "And he'd just lost a job that had meant a lot to him. That was another danger signal I should have picked up on."

"People do lose jobs. It happens fairly often."

"Yes, and this wasn't the first job Andrew was fired from. But his depression hit him harder this time. He even—he even forgot our anniversary, which he'd never done before."

Casey found that he hated the idea of Jackie having an anniversary with another man. *Grow up, Guthrie,* he counseled himself. "Jackie, it happens. From what I hear at work, men are always getting into trouble for stuff like that."

"But Andrew was very thoughtful that way. He made a big deal about my birthday and other special holidays. I should have known something was seriously wrong when he let our anniversary pass without a word."

"Did you say anything to him about it?"

"A week later I brought up the subject. Andrew felt terrible. He promised we'd go out for dinner. 'Next week,' he said. Only by the next week Andrew was—"

Jackie put her free hand to her face and Casey swung her into his arms. "It's okay, honey," he said. Woefully inadequate words, he knew, but Jackie didn't seem to care. She burrowed her face into his shoulder and he was so grateful to have the opportunity just to hold her.

And that seemed to be all she wanted. At first. Then her hand came up to brush his hair back from his forehead. She looked at him with something like longing, and dampened her lips.

For the first time in his life, he felt like a babe in the woods when it came to a woman. He wasn't sure what Jackie wanted from him right now and he ached to get this right. He'd made enough false steps with her.

For several minutes he agonized about whether she wanted him to kiss her. And then she surprised him by doing exactly that. She leaned forward and placed her lips softly on his, like a gift.

"Jackie?"

"Do you want to kiss me?"

He cupped her face with his hand. "Oh, yeah."

"Then do, Casey. I'm tired of crying on your shoulders."

"Well, technically, I don't think you *were* crying." At least he hadn't noticed any tears or sobs. Not this time.

"You know what I mean. I've turned into a basket case on you twice so far."

"I've got broad shoulders."

"You certainly do."

"I'm glad you noticed. And I want you to notice something else, too. I wasn't complaining."

"No. I wonder why."

"I think I gave you the answer to that last night." He held his breath, afraid he might have scared her off again. Instead she put her lips next to his for a second kiss. This time he didn't need any more hints about what she craved. He shifted his weight and the angle of his face so he could kiss her back.

Really kiss her back. The kind of kiss that let her know exactly how much he wanted her.

When she moaned, he knew he'd got it right.

"Can we find someplace a little more…comfortable?" Jackie asked.

Casey laid his jacket over the grass behind the log. They were sheltered here by low-growing shrubs, so if anyone did happen by, they wouldn't see anything. Well, not much, anyway.

Jackie cuddled up next to him and they laughed like kids who knew they were doing something wrong, but hey, it was such damn fun.

He slid his hands under the bulkiness of her sweater to find her lovely, soft skin. He ran his fingers up the length of her back, then held her close to his chest, treasuring her nearness.

Jackie nuzzled her face against his neck. He felt her warm, gentle kisses creep along the line of his jaw, and he moaned when she bypassed his mouth in favor of the other side of his face.

As she leaned up and over him, he was able to explore more of her body. Her flat tummy, the gentle swell of her breasts beneath the lacy cups.

It was heaven to touch her. And when she'd finished her hot little kisses, he worked to claim all he had touched with kisses of his own. His fingers brushed against a zipper at the side of her skirt.

"Yes," she whispered encouragingly, pulling her sweater over her shoulders as he tugged off her skirt. He unfastened her bra, leaving her with nothing but skimpy silk panties.

She was not at all self-conscious about being nearly naked in broad daylight in a public park. Her boldness made him unbearably hot, and he slid his fingers beneath the fabric of her damp panties.

"Yes," she whispered again as he eased them down her long, luscious legs.

And then it was his turn to undress. He used his T-shirt to cushion her head. His jeans landed in a heap by her sweater.

"Casey, you're in amazingly good shape." She trailed her hands down his chest to his hard belly, back to his shoulders. "I can't get over how beautiful your body is." Jackie touched him everywhere, her feathery touch driving him wild.

"Honey, you're stealing all my lines." He held her close for one more kiss, thrilling in the sensation of her body pressed along the length of his own.

He'd had sex with a lot of women—not as many as some people might think, but still, a lot of women. But not until this moment had he realized that the act of making love could be about more than pleasure and having fun.

It could heal, too. And comfort.

"Are you sure, Jackie? Is this okay? Would you rather I took you home?"

"I can see the blue sky and hear the wind in the trees and the ocean in the background. This is perfect, Casey."

"You're perfect." He had protection with him, and he took care of that. Then he moved over her, kissing the smile from her face as he eased himself inside of her.

"This feels so right, Casey."

"That's what I've been saying from the start, hon." He started to move and felt her right there with him. Staring into the warmth of her eyes, he knew she was entirely his at this moment.

And he planned to make her his forever.

SINCE HIS LAST VISIT from the cop and the nurse, Wallace Voltz's anxiety had continued to escalate. His efforts to get more information—information he desperately needed—had been stonewalled. As a last resort, he'd begged his son to hire a bodyguard for Haley, but Bill had flat out refused.

His son, Wallace had noticed, was becoming increasingly defiant these days. Perhaps it was time to have a little chat and remind him where his monthly stipend came from.

In fact, that was a damn good idea. Wallace strode into the piano room, where Abigail was playing a Beethoven sonata with dreadful accuracy. He stopped her midphrase.

"I'm going to drop in on Bill and Sherri-Ann. Would you like to come with me?"

She lifted her fingers from the keys. "Tonight?"

"That's right. I'd like to see Haley. They aren't bringing her around as often as before."

"I think the kidnapping spooked Sherri-Ann. She hasn't been going out at all. I can't say that I blame her. That was always my worst nightmare—that someone would abduct Billy."

It annoyed Wallace when his wife spoke of their son as if he were a child instead of a grown man. If she hadn't coddled him so much when he was younger, perhaps Wallace would have had more luck trying to establish a relationship with the boy.

He wasn't going to make that mistake with Haley. Just thinking of the tiny, sweet baby had him yearning to hold her.

"Would you like to leave right after dinner, Wallace?"

"No. Now."

She looked at him as if he'd suggested taking an ax to the street and randomly attacking people. "But, Wallace. We can't go visiting during the dinner hour. That would be rude."

"Nevertheless, that's what I'm going to do. We haven't seen Haley since we brought her home from the hospital, even though we're footing the bill for everything over there from the new car to twenty-four-hour nursing."

Abigail's face turned still and pale. "Do you think something's wrong?"

After years of protecting his wife from the seamier side of family relations, Wallace finally gave up.

"Yes, I do," he said.

Abigail closed the piano lid with a thud. "Then I'm coming, too. Wait while I get my hat and purse."

Wallace paced in the foyer, car keys jangling in his hand. "Hurry up, Abigail," he called, after yet another impatient glance at his watch.

He was about to race upstairs and drag his wife out of their bedroom, when the telephone rang. For a moment he considered letting the service answer, then reconsidered and picked up the receiver.

"Voltz residence."

"Is this Wallace Voltz speaking?"

His heart felt as if it had stopped beating. In fact, he wished for a moment that it really would. He knew the voice on the other end of the line—would recognize it anywhere, even though he'd heard it only once before in his life.

"Yes," he managed to reply, his throat constricted with dread. "What do you want?"

THOUGH SHE WAS ANXIOUS to see Haley, Jackie was not looking forward to another visit with Bill and Sherri-Ann Voltz. As Casey kept telling her, though, this was a reconnaissance mission, not a social visit. Their number-one priority was to make sure Haley was okay. Any information they were able to glean from the younger Voltz couple would be considered bonus points.

They'd stopped off at both their apartments to change clothes after their impromptu lovemaking. Now they had to hurry to make their five-o'clock appointment, but Jackie didn't mind. She smiled. She was glad that her first time with Casey had happened outside, on the beach. It seemed fitting somehow.

They stopped quickly at the library to prepare for the meeting ahead. Still giggling like teenagers, they checked microfiche records for everything recent they could find on the Voltz family.

Most of the clippings had to do with Wallace

Voltz's charitable activities, but there'd been an announcement of Bill and Sherri-Ann's engagement as well as a brief report of the wedding in the society pages. The event had been a traditional high-society extravaganza, and Sherri-Ann's expression in the black-and-white photo was one teetering between delight and triumph.

Jackie was reminded of Casey's comment when he'd first met the couple. If Sherri-Ann had anticipated living in style after marrying Bill Voltz, she must have been crushed by the reality.

Wallace Voltz expected his son to make his own way in life. But was that fair when his own fortune had come courtesy of his wife?

The most recent newspaper clipping they'd found had been the announcement of Haley Abigail Voltz's birth. Here again, Jackie saw evidence of both delight and triumph. Clearly, Haley had been a much anticipated, much loved child.

And two months later she'd been kidnapped.

From the library they drove directly to Bill and Sherri-Ann's. "Looks like it's going to be a cocktail party," Casey commented as he pulled up to the side of the road. Already parked in the driveway was the senior Voltz's gleaming burgundy Rolls-Royce.

"Oh, joy. We get to visit with the entire family," Jackie said.

Casey eased his car behind a neighbor's overgrown hedge, then came around to open Jackie's door. This was the first time she'd seen him dressed up, and she loved the way his dark sweater outlined his powerful torso and broad shoulders. Casey, she'd decided, was not as much handsome as he was sexy. Tonight, though, he looked both.

She couldn't stop herself from thinking that this was going to be a dangerous night. In more ways than one.

The door opened as soon as Casey rang the bell.

Sherri-Ann, in designer jeans and a low-cut T-shirt, gaped at them in the manner of someone who was truly caught off guard.

Jackie and Casey exchanged uncomfortable glances. "Did we get the wrong afternoon?" Jackie asked. "Bill did say Friday at five, didn't he?"

"Oh, Lord. I can't believe we forgot."

Under normal circumstances Jackie would have beat a hasty retreat and tried to spare Sherri-Ann any additional embarrassment. But as Casey had already established, this was a reconnaissance mission, not a social occasion.

She and Casey stood their ground, while Sherri-Ann shot a distressed look behind her. "Look, Bill. It's Officer Guthrie and Nurse Kellison."

A very inelegant expletive was expelled with enough volume to be heard clearly on the landing. Jackie clamped down on the urge to smile.

By the time Bill appeared, Casey had maneuvered her into the foyer, with the front door shut firmly behind them. Sherri-Ann had a puzzled frown on her face as if she couldn't quite figure out how that had happened.

Jackie was learning a lot from Casey about worming her way into places she wasn't wanted—a skill she hoped she wouldn't need very often in the future.

"I'm so sorry," Bill said, rushing forward, as if trying to contain them in the foyer. "We completely forgot about our invitation. I hope you don't mind if we postpone until another day. We've been so busy with Haley—we aren't prepared for company…"

How busy could they be, given that they were supposed to have a nurse on the premises around the clock?

"No problem." Casey sounded relaxed and self-assured as he leaned an arm against the railing that divided foyer from sitting area. "These mix-ups happen."

"No doubt." Bill's anxiety was clearly mounting. "Look, I never did offer you a reward for what you did for Haley. There's a lovely restaurant in our neighborhood—you may have noticed on your drive in. We have an account with the manager. Why don't I give him a call and have him set up a nice table for two…"

"Oh, we're not at all hungry," Casey lied. "Besides, we couldn't accept any reward for doing our jobs."

"Well, then." Bill glanced at the door in a heavy hint that they should just please *leave.* At that moment his mother entered the room from the kitchen.

"Bill." Abigail's tone was sharp. "Stop talking all that nonsense and tell them what happened."

"Mother," Bill replied in a warning tone.

Then, surprisingly, Wallace came up from behind his wife. "Listen to your mother, Bill. We can trust these two. They saved Haley once. They're not going to do or say anything to hurt her. In fact, I don't see that we have any choice but to confide in them."

Jackie's heart was sinking already. She and Casey had been right to be worried. "Has Haley been kidnapped again?"

For a long moment there was silence. Sherri-Ann glared across the room at her husband. Bill stared at his feet, while Wallace and Abigail clung to each other.

"I'm afraid so," Wallace finally said. "She was snatched from her crib this afternoon when she was taking her nap."

"How is that possible?" Jackie wondered if these people were imbeciles.

"Apparently neither the window nor the security system had been properly repaired from the last time," Abigail said, showing uncharacteristic displeasure toward her son. "Really, Bill," she added. "How could you be so negligent?"

"Where was the nurse all this time?" Casey wondered.

Bill and Sherri-Ann wouldn't look at him.

"My son dispensed with her services after the first day," Wallace said, his tone clipped, "and pocketed the money that had been intended to pay her wages."

"We didn't need her," Bill said in his defense. "Sherri-Ann and I had no trouble managing the medications and changing the dressings. It was a waste—"

Jackie could not believe they would be so careless. "Have you phoned the police yet?"

"No, and you can't, either," Bill said quickly.

"Dad received a phone call a couple of hours after Haley disappeared. We can't contact the police. It's too dangerous for our baby. We have to keep quiet and pay the ransom. That's the only chance we have of getting Haley back alive."

Abigail started to cry then, while Sherri-Ann looked angrier than ever.

"Is this how Haley was kidnapped the first time?" Casey asked. "Snatched through her bedroom window?"

"Yes," Wallace said. "Only it happened at night. The kidnapper cut through the glass and screening of her window, and also managed to disable the security system. Bill and Sherri-Ann didn't realize she was missing until her 2:00 a.m. feeding."

Casey noticed no one was bothering to pretend that the first kidnapping hadn't taken place.

"I can't stand this, Wallace." Abigail sniffed into a delicate hanky. "Why does this keep happening to our family?"

Wallace slipped a comforting arm around his wife. "We'll get her back, Abigail. I swear we will." He caught Bill's gaze and a powerful anger traveled from father to son.

Bill turned to his mother. "We're going to need another three million, Mom."

"Oh, Billy…"

"And I hope you're not going to drag your feet this time like you did before. You and Dad value your investment portfolio more than your own granddaughter."

"That isn't fair, Billy." Abigail's tone was sharp. "You have no idea how complicated it is to gather a sum like three million dollars."

"All the banks have transaction reporting rules to contend with," her husband added. "Last time we had to call in a favor from a business associate who owns a casino in Las Vegas. We wired him $3.3 million in exchange for a suitcase with $3 million in cash. No way can we get away with doing something like that again."

"We don't have the liquid investments anyway." Abigail glanced at Casey and Jackie. "We live off an income trust—I'm not allowed to touch the capital in my lifetime. Our house is worth three million or more, but it would take months to sell."

"Did the kidnapper give you a time limit to come up with the money?" Casey asked.

Wallace nodded. "Twenty-four hours. I'm afraid it's impossible."

"It can't be impossible." Bill raked a hand through his hair, standing his cowlick on end. "Just ask yourself how much you love Haley."

He moved away from his parents, and as he turned in her direction, Jackie noticed that his hair wasn't standing up because of a cowlick at all. He had a row of stitches on his hairline and they didn't look very old.

"What happened?" she asked, gesturing to the wound.

He waved a hand dismissively. "Bumped my head on a door."

"You know we love Haley—more than anything,"

Wallace said, continuing the conversation. "But it simply isn't possible to put together another three million in twenty-four hours. We have to stall this woman somehow."

"Dear God." Sherri-Ann held out her hands, her face pale. "I can't stand to talk about this anymore." She fled downstairs, and after a few seconds, her husband followed.

Suddenly the room became very quiet.

"What should we do?"

Abigail asked the question to no one in particular, but it was Casey who answered.

"You stay by the phone and try not to panic. I have a few ideas I'd like to check out. But before I do, I think your husband has a secret he can no longer afford to keep. What do you say, Wallace? Will you tell your wife? Or should I?"

CHAPTER FOURTEEN

AT FIRST Wallace tried to bluff his way out of the situation. "I don't have a clue what you're talking about."

Casey almost exploded. "Look, I don't know what games you and your family are playing, but I'm getting fed up with them."

Jackie had to agree. She counted three separate times she and Casey had listened to Wallace spin various stories to explain the strange happenings in his family.

"Officer Guthrie, I'm sure your interest in my family began as a kindhearted concern about my granddaughter, but frankly, your behavior has escalated beyond—"

"Wallace?" Abigail prodded her husband's back. "You always speak that way when you're trying to hide something. What is it?"

Abruptly, Wallace's highhanded manner fell to the wayside as he sank to the sofa in the living room. Ignoring his wife and guests, he cupped his head in his hands. Abigail sat beside him, her back ramrod-stiff.

"You've got to level with us, Wallace," Casey said. "We don't have time for any more of your lies."

Silently, Jackie went to a tray that had been left on a table by some bookshelves and poured two glasses of water. She offered them to Wallace and Abigail, then glanced at Casey, who had positioned himself in a challenging stance in front of the older couple, arms crossed over his powerful chest.

The moment he noticed her looking at him, she thought his mouth twitched in an almost imperceptible smile. It didn't take her long to realize what was amusing him.

We're doing the good cop/bad cop routine. He was being tough and hard, while she'd naturally fallen into the sympathetic role of ally. If the situation hadn't been so dire, she would have been amused, too. As it was, she waited breathlessly to see what Casey would say next.

"Okay, no more bull from you, Mr. Voltz. Let's talk about how this whole situation started."

Wallace nodded. "I guess you're right. It's confession time." He put a hand on Abigail's knee. "I'm so sorry, darling. I never wanted you to know."

What little color had been left in his wife's face now disappeared. "What, Wallace?"

Her husband stared at the opposite wall, disconsolate.

Casey prodded him. "Tell her about the affair. It's better coming from you."

"Affair?" Abigail's voice was shrill.

"I'm afraid it's true." Wallace sighed. "Our

Bill's been cheating on Sherri-Ann for almost a year now."

"*Bill's* been cheating?" Jackie couldn't contain her astonishment. "We thought you were the one having the affair."

Wallace looked amazed. "I've never been unfaithful to Abigail. My father slept around on my mother and it tore our family apart. I swore I'd never make that mistake. But I'm afraid my son was not so wise. I have the reports from an investigator to prove this."

"You spied on our son?"

"I'm sorry, Abby. I suspected he was up to no good. I felt I could better protect the family if I knew exactly what he was doing. Unfortunately, I failed to prevent this disaster." His shoulders sank forward in a posture of defeat.

"I'm not sure I understand." Abigail had her hand at her throat again. "What does Bill's affair have to do with Haley?" Her nostrils compressed as she took a fortifying breath. "It was the woman who died, wasn't it? That Rosie Thatcher. She was Bill's lover. And she stole our granddaughter."

"Yes—" Casey and Jackie began speaking in unison, but Wallace interrupted them.

"No. All three of you are wrong. Rosie wasn't Bill's mistress. It was her sister. Theresa."

THERESA. Beautiful, exotic Theresa was Bill—not Wallace—Voltz's lover. It took a few minutes before Casey was sure he had it straight.

Abigail Voltz invited them back to the kitchen,

where she brewed a pot of coffee. The four of them—Jackie, Casey, Wallace and Abigail—drank until the pot was empty. And talked.

"I know it must be my fault somehow." Wallace stared into his empty mug. "But I never could get close to my son."

Abigail reached across the table to touch his hand. "I let him come running to me when he had a disagreement with you. I see now that was a mistake."

Slowly the Voltzes tried to sort through the wheres and whys of how they'd gone wrong with their only son. Finally, Casey had to remind them what was really important here.

"Do you think it's possible Theresa Thatcher has Haley right now?"

Everyone fell silent.

"That makes sense," Jackie said at last. "Remember how strange she was when we talked to her this morning, Casey? She probably had the second kidnapping planned and we were interrupting her timetable."

"We've been wondering from the start who Rosie's partner could have been," Casey told Wallace and Abigail. "We thought it might have been Rosie's lover, but now it turns out she didn't have the lover—Theresa did. So doesn't it make sense that Theresa enlisted her sister's aid in the kidnapping? And that Theresa—not Rosie—was behind both of the abductions?"

"Oh, Wallace, I can't think straight anymore." Abigail put her hands to her temples. "We have to get Haley back. What should we do—go to the police?"

"I don't know." Wallace sounded worried. "She told us if we went to the police we'd never see Haley again."

Casey sat silently, warring with his conscience. In the past week he'd broken with police procedure several times already. He knew that to do his job properly, he had to insist they report this crime. But was that the safest for Haley?

He noticed Jackie eyeing him anxiously. She understood the dilemma he was facing. In that instant he made up his mind.

"The first step is to find Theresa. She knows Jackie and me. She won't be suspicious if we drop by her apartment again." That would be safer than sending the police, Casey was sure. "Once we establish exactly where your granddaughter is, we'll be better prepared to act."

"You would do that for us?" Abigail asked.

"We'd do it for Haley," Casey gently corrected her.

WALLACE AND ABIGAIL had been very grateful for Casey's offer and Jackie had agreed it was the smartest plan. She leaned back in the passenger seat of the Saab. Casey had put up the roof. The sky was dark and foreboding and it had started to rain—enough to sprinkle them with moisture as they'd run out the front door to the car.

"Casey, do you think we should call your brother and let him know what's happened?"

"We don't have time to set those wheels in motion, Jackie. Besides, do you really think the Voltz family will cooperate any better this time than the last? I'll end up looking like a fool again, which I wouldn't mind if I thought it would help Haley, but actually, I think the end result might be the opposite. If Theresa sees that the police are involved, she may panic and do the very thing we don't want her to do."

"Oh, Casey. I hate to say this, but what you're suggesting makes sense. We've got to consider Haley's safety first."

"At least you and I have a semi-legitimate excuse to call on Theresa. We can ask for details of Rosie's funeral, or simply say that we wanted to stop by to make sure she's okay. If we play it cool, she'll never know that we've been told about the kidnapping."

"That evil woman. I can't believe I felt sorry for her. She played us for fools that first time we met her. Claiming her sister might have been hired as a baby-sitter, when she was the one who'd roped Rosie into looking after the baby that she herself had kid-napped."

"Yeah, and then she played all innocent about the stolen car… I keep thinking about those rope burns. They have to fit into the equation somehow. But I can't come up with any logical explanation."

"Poor Rosie." Jackie was back to feeling sorry for the young woman killed in the terrible car crash. "I wonder how involved she was in this plan?"

"We may never know." Casey slowed as they passed a fast-food drive-in. "We haven't eaten since breakfast. What do you say we pick up something here?"

Jackie was surprised to find that despite all the trauma and excitement, she was starving. She decided on a double burger with cheese, while Casey ordered the same with added bacon.

Unwrapping the fragrant sandwich, she inhaled with pleasure. "You know, we've got to stop eating like this. It's very bad for our cholesterol."

"Welcome to the life of a cop. We usually don't have time to order a meal at a regular restaurant."

"Something else your job has in common with mine. I try to pack healthy snacks, but when I'm busy, I end up eating from the vending machine a lot."

"Maybe one day we could take a cooking course together."

"I've got a better idea. You take the course. I'll sample the results."

Casey shot her a teasing grin and she felt her heart lift with happiness. She loved joking with him this way, loved even more the implied assumption that they would be spending time together in the future.

Casey Guthrie was a man of action. Strong-minded. Determined.

Andrew had been none of those things, and though it wasn't fair to compare, she realized that she'd been the dominant person in that relationship on many levels. She'd been the primary wage-earner as well as homemaker. And she'd been the one to provide a shoulder for both strength and comfort during Andrew's emotional ups and downs.

She suspected Casey wouldn't want, or need, a

woman to look after him the way she'd looked after Andrew. The idea that she could be with a man and still have some freedom, some breathing room— some *fun*—was exciting.

In his sleek sweater and fitted trousers, Casey looked outrageously sexy. His brown hair had gone a little curly with the rain and his handsome profile was set in determination.

Jackie wanted to kiss him something awful.

Not good timing, she told herself, then grabbed onto the side of her seat as Casey abruptly pulled the car to the side of the road.

"If you're going to look at me like that, there will be consequences." And then he kissed her.

"How many consequences do we have time for?" She did her best to replicate the look she'd given him before.

He kissed her again, then growled in her ear. "We have to stop this. There's a baby girl who needs our help."

"Good point." She smoothed down her hair and straightened her jacket. Haley was only a couple of months old and already she'd been snatched from her home on two occasions. Jackie hoped Theresa was taking good care of the infant. She hoped Haley truly was too young to feel frightened and alone.

"How aware is a baby at Haley's age?" Casey asked, obviously thinking along the same lines.

"Well, she's old enough to recognize her primary caregivers—in Haley's case, her mom and dad. Maybe her grandparents, too, since it sounds as if they've spent a fair amount of time with her. In terms of her physical development, she may be starting to have some control over her hands, and smiling."

Casey sighed. "I hope to God she doesn't remember any of this when she's older." He eased off the accelerator as they approached Theresa's apartment.

Jackie gazed out at the lighted windows. Only a few remained dark. "I have a feeling she isn't going to be here."

"Theresa probably isn't at Rosie's, either. Still, I feel we should try both places."

Jackie agreed. It wouldn't do to overlook the obvious.

Just as they'd expected, there was no answer at either apartment, and none of the neighbors they questioned had seen a woman matching Theresa's description with a baby.

In frustration they returned to the car. "You know, Theresa could be anywhere in the city," Casey said. "We'd be better off keeping an eye on Bill. I don't trust that guy. I think he might sneak off to meet her. Try to work out a special deal with his ex-lover."

"And when he does, we follow him...straight to Haley."

Casey dropped a light punch on her shoulder. "That's exactly right, partner. Now, ever been on a stakeout before?"

"Let me think." She pretended to give the question some consideration. "Um, no, I don't believe so."

"Okay, then. Sit back, watch and learn. First stop is a convenience store. We need to stock up."

THEY PREPARED for their stakeout in grand style. Chocolate and an extra-large latte for Jackie. Spicy nachos and a super-size Coke for Casey. They both agreed on donuts for dessert.

"You need dessert after chocolate?" Casey asked.

"You have a problem with that?"

"Not a bit." Casey pulled up to Bill Voltz's house for the second time that night. First thing he noticed was that the Rolls was missing.

"So Abigail and Wallace have gone home."

"That's probably wise, since the kidnapper seems to prefer phoning their house."

"Theresa knows who controls the purse strings in the family."

After parking behind the same bush as earlier, Casey turned off the ignition and gave thanks it was a dark night. It was still raining outside, making the car interior cozy and warm. He pushed aside the bags of snack food to slide his hand around Jackie's shoulder. "Maybe we shouldn't have bought any food at all. I can think of better ways to spend our time."

He let a finger slide under the collar of her pullover. She felt a tingle down her entire torso as he caressed that single inch of skin.

"You're right. That *is* a good idea. But is this a good time? I know I'm the novice here, but during a stakeout, isn't it important to keep an eye on the mark?"

"It turns me on when you use police lingo, Jackie."

He placed his lips where his finger had been. *In-*

finitely better. Sadly, he pulled back just when he was beginning to make some interesting progress.

"But you're right," he said. "We'd better pay attention to what we're doing. Which means junk food, not sex."

Jackie tore open her first fruit-and-nut chocolate bar. She broke off a square and placed it in her mouth to savor. She went still when she noticed Casey watching her.

"So, you're a melt-in-the-mouth kind of girl?"

"Pretty much." She sipped at the latte. Mmm. The rich bitter coffee and sweet nutty chocolate made the perfect combination. "You know, I could get used to this kind of life. Maybe I should become a detective."

"We could start our own agency. You know, like Bruce Willis and Cybil Sheppard in 'Moonlighting.'"

"The couple who were always fighting?"

"They did some other stuff, too, as I recall."

Yeah, he would remember that. But to be honest, so did she. The simmering romance between the two protagonists was the reason she'd watched so many of the reruns.

"Tell me more about your family, Casey. Your mom and dad. What are they like?"

"Well, they're nice."

She laughed. "That sounds pretty traditional."

"That's exactly what we are. Mom and Dad gave us such a grounded childhood, Adam and I never really had a chance to turn out twisted. I came closer than he did, though."

"Really? What's the worst thing you ever did?"

"Truthfully?" He sighed. "My reputation is much wilder than the reality. I may have broken a few hearts unnecessarily. I guess that's bad enough, huh?"

Not *too* bad. As long as hers wasn't one of them.

"Now you tell me something, Jackie."

"What do want to know?"

"Whether you could see yourself settling down again? With a guy like me."

"I'd like to get married, eventually. I definitely want children. But I don't know about marrying a cop. I was thinking something more in the line of an accountant. Maybe a dentist."

"Good God. Why?"

She laughed at how appalled he sounded. "I'm not sure I could handle the excitement of being a cop's wife."

"Are you kidding? You could never handle the boredom of being a regular guy's wife. That's what you could never handle."

Was it possible Casey was right?

"You know, Jackie, I may not be a cop much longer."

"Oh?"

"I don't want to stay on traffic patrol forever. And I'm not sure where else I could go."

"Have you thought of applying for detective? You have a flair for investigating."

"I do like working on a puzzle, trying to get to the bottom of a problem. But there are a lot of rules and regulations when you're a cop. And I've broken quite a few of them these past few days. I'm thinking I might be better off being my own boss."

"You mean, start your own P.I. firm?"

He nodded. "If I could make a viable living. I mean, I'd have to do some research…"

A dog barked and they both sat up straight. Jackie snapped off a second piece of chocolate and let her gaze drift back to Bill and Sherri-Ann's house. The only light was from a bedroom in the back.

"Casey, what if Bill never leaves and the kidnapper never calls? What if Haley is already…" She couldn't actually say the final word.

"All of that is possible. We just have to do what we can do. I gave Wallace and Abigail my cell phone number. If they receive a call, they know to phone me right away. In the meantime, we keep an eye on Bill and Sherri-Ann. I think it's the best anyone can do in the circumstances."

"Do you ever get scared on the job?"

He took her hand. "If I run into a situation that makes me uncomfortable, I call for backup."

He looked at her more closely. "What's the matter, Jackie? Are you feeling nervous about this?"

When she didn't respond, he drew his own conclusions. "I'll call you a cab. You can be home in twenty minutes…"

She stopped his hand from reaching for his cell phone.

"I want to be with you," she said quietly.

"Because you're worried about Haley?"

"That, too."

He squeezed her hand tightly. "One day we can tell our children that I won your heart by taking you on a stakeout."

No, he'd won her heart in other, more important ways. By seeing her, the real Jackie, and not wanting her to be anything else. By doing what he thought was best for Haley Voltz tonight instead of following standard police procedure. By loving her the way she'd waited a lifetime to be loved.

Casey looked at her deeply, his eyes full of all sorts of forever-after promises that Jackie suddenly realized she desperately wanted to believe in.

"One day soon I'll take you on a proper date," he said. "Dinner, wine, dancing…"

Seduction.

"That sounds nice. But don't think I haven't enjoyed our fast-food junkets and bombing around in your Saab."

He chuckled. "I do know how to show a girl a good time, don't I?" Leaning back in his seat, he yawned, his gaze flicking to the Voltz home, then away.

"Jackie, my next shift starts tomorrow morning. How about you?"

"I have another three days off," she reminded him. Thanks to the generosity of Dr. Callie Baker.

"Our wild hours are beginning to catch up to me and I don't like to start a shift exhausted. How about we take turns napping? You can go first."

"I don't feel tired." Maybe it was the coffee and the chocolate. More likely the situation and the company were to blame. "You're the one who has to go to work in the morning. You take the first nap."

"You'll wake me when you start to feel sleepy?"

"I will."

"Okay." He reclined his seat and closed his eyes. Jackie watched him covertly for several minutes, glancing periodically at the house to make sure nothing was happening.

Just when she was sure Casey had fallen asleep, he opened one eye.

"Don't eat all the donuts, okay?" Then he shifted in his seat and didn't speak again for several hours.

CASEY HAD BROUGHT ALONG a portable CD player with headphones and Jackie listened to that for a while. She drank all her latte and ate most of the chocolate. After that she was too full to eat even one donut.

She kept a close eye on the Voltz house. A couple of times she saw dark shadows pass across the bedroom windows, then at about midnight, all the lights in the house went out.

She shifted in her seat and checked Casey. He seemed to be deep in sleep and she marveled at his ability to drop off so quickly and sleep so soundly in such an uncomfortable setting.

In slumber, he looked adorable. She had to exercise great restraint not to touch him. *I guess this counts as our second night spent together.*

So far, they'd slept one night on her apartment floor, now in a car. They'd made love on the beach, then later in the shower getting cleaned up. Were the two of them ever going to actually make love and then sleep in a bed?

She smiled, thinking there was something special about having such a weird beginning to their relationship.

A yawn suddenly overtook her and Jackie stretched her arms above her head. Maybe she *should* switch roles with Casey and have a little power nap. She was reaching for Casey's shoulder to give him a jostle, when a light flashed on in the house.

Grabbing his arm, she shook him harder than she'd intended. He awoke instantly.

"What's up?"

"A light just came on." She pointed to the house. "It could be that one of them is having trouble sleeping, but—"

The sound of the garage door opening automatically cut her off. She watched as Bill stepped into the lighted garage. Quickly he slid into the driver's seat of the Audi and began to back out to the street.

Casey lowered the car windows as the front door of the house cracked open. Through the tangle of branches between them, Jackie could make out Sherri-Ann's silhouette on the landing.

Bill stopped the car and ran back to talk to his wife.

Despite the rain, Sherri-Ann's voice carried clearly through the night air.

"I swear, Bill, I don't care what trouble I get into. I'm going to call the cops if you don't come back with my baby."

"*Our* baby," he replied bitterly.

"And whatever you do, don't give her all three million." Sherri-Ann stepped back so that her husband could reach inside the house. He grabbed a large, obviously heavy suitcase.

"It's outrageous that she would ask for the whole cut," Sherri-Ann continued. Then she stepped back inside and slammed the door shut.

In amazement, Jackie watched Bill lug the suitcase to his car.

"What's Bill doing with the money?" Jackie whispered as she watched him stow it in the trunk. *Imagine, three million dollars...* "Do you think he got another three million from his father?"

"You heard Wallace and Abigail. There hasn't been enough time. My guess is this is the original payment."

"But he was supposed to have left that for the kidnapper, wasn't he?"

"That's what he claimed." Casey watched the receding lights of the Audi as Bill took off out of the neighborhood. When he judged the time was right, Casey shot out after him.

Jackie sat on her hands, her entire body trembling.

After hours of waiting, finally something was happening. And from the sounds of Bill and Sherri-Ann's conversation, it was going to be very interesting.

CHAPTER FIFTEEN

WALLACE VOLTZ WOKE from his fitful sleep, certain that someone—Haley? Bill?—was in dire danger. He glanced across at Abigail. She'd taken a sedative earlier and was now lying flat on her back, a mask over her eyes, her face calm and pale. He leaned in close enough to hear the gentle wheezing of her breath, then, reassured that she was all right, slipped out of the king-size bed and grabbed his robe.

Actually his wife had handled everything that had happened today with more strength than he had imagined she possessed. Maybe he'd underestimated her all these years.

A glance at the clock on the bedside table told him it was a few minutes past three in the morning. He rubbed his hand over his face, feeling the grizzle of his morning beard.

God, that had been a terrible dream.

Should he take a pill and try to go back to bed? As quickly as the idea came to him, he discarded it. No medication was going to lull him back to sleep this night. Besides, he didn't want to take the risk of sleeping through an important call.

He went to the window, steamy from the drizzle outside, and wondered where in the world his beloved granddaughter was right now.

It seemed natural to go to the room he and Abigail had prepared for her when she was born. Right from the start, they'd hoped to be involved grandparents. They'd dreamed of having Haley for weekends and holidays when her parents needed a break.

Swathed in white eyelet and lace, the nursery was a romantic, pretty room. All too empty now. He picked up one of the soft blankets from the crib and brought it to his face. Closing his eyes, he inhaled the sweet scent of baby.

Haley, his heart cried. *Where are you?*

"I CAN'T FIGURE OUT where the hell he's going," Casey muttered, taking another corner in blind pursuit of the Audi.

Jackie sympathized with Casey's frustration. He was doing an excellent job of following Bill, who was driving so erratically he must have been drinking or was incredibly nervous.

"Well, he isn't headed to Theresa's apartment— or Rosie's," she said, stating the obvious. They'd passed the turnoffs to both those neighborhoods. Now they were winding their way through a middle-class community with property values a notch below those in Bill and Sherri-Ann's area.

They passed a church. The Orange Grove United. Then turned down a wide boulevard with houses divided by a median of young palm trees. Bill careened around the corner so fast his tires squealed. Then he overcompensated by taking the next turn at a crawl.

As they entered a school zone the Audi first sped up, then slowed again. Jackie focused on the low building to her left. Streetlamps illuminated a sign at the front of the building. Orange Grove Nursery School.

"Wait a minute, Casey. Isn't that where Theresa works?"

Her hunch was proven correct as the Audi took a final turn into the deserted parking lot. Casey hung back on the street, swinging into a residential cul-de-sac where his vehicle wouldn't attract attention. He cut the motor.

Using his cell phone, he dialed dispatch at his station house. "Hey, Amanda. Working the night shift?"

Amanda. Jackie wrinkled her nose at Casey. *Another old girl friend?* He gave her a mollifying smile.

"Look, I was out late and noticed a guy driving a little erratically. He's pulled into a nursery school parking lot and I'd like someone to come check him out." Casey relayed the exact address. "Better warn the guys that this could turn out to be something big. If my hunch is right, we may have a kidnapper on our hands."

There was a pause, undoubtedly filled with questions, but Casey cut Amanda off. "Sorry, but I don't have time to get into it right now. I'm going in to keep an eye on the situation."

He disconnected the phone and tossed it into the back of the car.

"Are they sending someone?"

"Yeah. It'll be fifteen minutes or so." He zipped on a waterproof coat and pulled up the hood. In the dark, he turned into a big, menacing shadow.

As he opened the door, Jackie pulled her jacket around her shoulders. "I'm coming, too."

"No, Jackie."

"What do you mean, no? I'm in this as much as you are."

"But I need you in the car. If you hear gunshots, stay low and call emergency. When the squad car gets here, fill the guys in on what's happening. I don't want anyone walking in at the wrong moment."

Jackie had fixated on the word *gunshots*. "You think Bill and Theresa have guns?"

"At this point I'll be surprised if they don't."

KEEPING LOW, Casey ran across the street, then crept behind a short hedge that followed the sidewalk up to the school. From the front he couldn't see any signs of occupancy, but as he moved stealthily toward the back of the building, he realized that a rear door—probably used for receiving supplies—had been opened. A faint light glowed from within. Too small to be from an electrical fixture, it was probably a flashlight. As he moved closer, his hunch was confirmed. He hid behind a large metal garbage bin beside the doorway and peered out.

Theresa sat on a wooden table in the darkened room, her jeans-clad legs swinging slightly. Not a sound came from the infant car seat by her side. She held a flashlight in one hand and in her other—a gun.

About ten feet in front of her stood Bill, his hands empty, the suitcase he'd brought from home on the floor.

"Okay, Theresa—" Bill's voice was low, cajoling "—I was wrong. I'm sorry. Can't you give me another chance?"

Theresa's lips curled scornfully. "My sister's dead and you want me to give you another chance?"

Casey wondered if Bill heard the same controlled fury in Theresa's voice that he did.

"You weren't meant to get Rosie involved."

"Well, how was I supposed to look after your baby while I was working?"

"Fine. But when I came with the money, the plan wasn't for Rosie to have Haley then."

"Rosie was my insurance policy, in case you double-crossed me. And you did, Bill—I have the rope burns to prove it."

"I'm sorry I had to tie you up. But your sister got me, too." He indicated the cut on his forehead. "After I left you, I went to her apartment. She knocked me out cold with a frying pan, the bitch."

"But you'd slashed her tires before you went up to her apartment."

"I thought it was smart to cut off her escape route. I'd never have guessed she had the nerve to steal a car. Why didn't she go to your place? The cops figure she was on the way to my old man's when she got into that accident."

"Rosie was freaked. She told me if one little thing went wrong, she was taking the baby back to her grandparents."

"What a bloody mess. You know, Theresa, if you'd just stuck to the plan…"

"Don't blame this on me! You told me you were going to leave Sherri-Ann. I should have known better than to trust you."

"I'm sorry, Theresa. I know I made a mistake."

"That was no mistake. It was your plan all along. You and Sherri-Ann thought you had it all figured out, didn't you? Did she know you were screwing me? Or did she think I was just some loser you were going to use to stage a fake kidnapping to get money out of your father…"

"Theresa, no! You were important to me. You still are. Come on, put the gun away. We can leave Haley here for the cops to take back to Sherri-Ann. Then you and I can run off to Canada like we planned."

Theresa's only response was to lift the weapon in her hand and level it at Bill's chest. It was a Saturday night special, Casey guessed. Great. He didn't have any weapons on him, since he wasn't on duty and hadn't anticipated anything like this when he'd left home.

"I wish I could believe you, Bill. But I don't. You still love Sherri-Ann."

"No, I swear… Look, Theresa, even if I wanted to stay with my wife, she'd never take me back. She's so pissed about the baby. She thought I was leaving her with my old elementary school English teacher.

When that cop and nurse came around with a picture of you and Rosie, she almost killed me. Then she almost killed me again when you snatched our baby for the second time."

"That sounds like your problem, Bill. Not mine."

"Come on, Theresa. Be fair."

"Fair? Is it fair that Rosie is dead? If you'd kept your end of the deal from the beginning, you and I would have had all that money. We could have started a new life in Canada, like we dreamed."

"You know, my kid almost died in that crash, too. That wasn't my fault."

"It was your fault Rosie's tires were slashed. Your fault she was too scared to come to me. Besides, don't try to convince me you really care about your kid. All you want is Daddy's money. Isn't that right, Billy?"

"I care about Haley. Come on, Theresa, let me see her."

"You can see her, fine. She's right here in her car seat. Sleeping like a baby, thanks to a dose of cough syrup I gave her about an hour ago."

"Jesus, Theresa! Are you crazy? Haley's too young for cough syrup. Sherri-Ann's going to kill me."

"Shut up about Sherri-Ann, will you? Why should I care about that bitch?"

"How much cough syrup did you give the baby?"

"I read the package, you idiot. I just wanted her to sleep for a while, that's all. What kind of monster do you think I am?"

"Of course I don't think you're a monster. I love

you, Theresa. Really. Now let's be calm and focus on our situation. So what do you want to do? Split the money fifty-fifty?"

"In your dreams, buddy. Why should I share anything with you? I've got the baby. I've got the gun."

"Theresa, be reasonable."

"I'm done with reasonable. I want my money. Take ten paces back from that suitcase. Do it now or I'm going to toss this car seat across the room. Then we'll both see whether I remembered to fasten the safety straps."

CHAPTER SIXTEEN

IT FELT LIKE FOREVER since Casey had left the car, but in actual fact, only seven minutes had passed. Jackie twisted the key to auxiliary power, then opened the windows. She couldn't hear any shouting, but the school was set back about forty feet from the street and she'd watched Casey walk to the back of the building.

The waiting was interminable. Jackie fidgeted in her seat as she strained to hear sounds from the dark nursery school. A couple times she thought she heard some muffled shouting, but the rain made it hard to be sure.

Maybe she should drive a little closer.

Sliding over to the driver's seat, she started the car and inched out of the cul-de-sac. She turned in front of the school and parked behind a black Accord.

Wait a minute. Didn't Theresa own an Accord? Jackie remembered seeing it parked in the hospital lot the day she and Casey had insisted on driving Theresa home.

Bill's Audi was in the parking lot on the other side of the street.

Hmm. What if she found a way to disable both Bill's and Theresa's vehicles? That way, when the squad car showed up, they wouldn't be able to make a run for it.

Turning up her collar against the rain, she ran lightly across the road to the Audi. The car was locked tight.

An idea occurred to her, and she smiled. It was very fitting.

She ran back to the Saab and got the penknife she'd noticed Casey kept in his glove compartment. She dashed back to the Audi, then with great satisfaction slashed gashes in each of Bill's four tires.

That had been ridiculously easy.

Next the Accord. As she approached the second vehicle, she heard something peculiar. A faint background noise that sounded like...a lullaby.

She picked up her pace, running to the parked vehicle. She recognized the song now—it was the Kenny Loggins's one about Pooh Corner. She cupped her hands over her forehead and peered in the window. Sure enough, in the center of the back seat was a rear-facing baby carrier with a blanket thrown over top.

Haley.

The front window of the vehicle was open several inches—probably for air circulation—but the doors were locked. Inside, she saw keys dangling from the ignition. Theresa must have left the car on auxiliary power so the tape player could operate.

Her heart was thumping so loudly now she

couldn't hear the music at all. Just to be sure, she tried the doors and confirmed they were locked. Next she eyed the open window again. Was her arm slender enough?

She tried to reach her hand in to touch the old-fashioned knob lock, but fell short by inches. The problem was that she had to bend her arm at the elbow. Maybe if she climbed on the roof and reached down, she could keep her arm straight…

In seconds Jackie was stepping up on the bumper, sliding over the hood, then climbing to the roof, the old metal heaving a little under her weight.

Reaching down, she eased her hand through the opening in the window and grasped for the knob. The hard plastic teased the ends of her fingers. Sliding forward slightly, she attempted the maneuver again, and this time was able to grip the knob and pull up.

She'd done it.

Jackie scrambled off the car and opened first the front door, then the rear one. She was about to lift the blanket off the carrier when she heard a shout from behind her.

She swiveled to find Bill and Theresa lugging the suitcase of money between them—and waving their fists at her.

"Get away from that car!" Bill shouted.

What the hell was going on? Where was Casey? Jackie had no clue. All she knew was that she wasn't letting either Bill or Theresa near this baby.

With one final glance at the car seat—she still

didn't know for sure if Haley was in there, but why would Bill and Theresa be after her if she wasn't?— Jackie slammed the back door shut then scuttled in behind the wheel. She started the engine with a quick turn of her fingers, then hit the gas pedal just as Bill and Theresa reached the street. They dropped the suitcase, waved their arms and yelled for her to stop, but she ignored them.

She ripped out of the neighborhood doing thirty miles over the legal limit and headed for the PCH.

CASEY MOANED AND ROLLED over on the wet grass. What the hell was he doing here?

The memories came back in dribbles. There'd been a gun. There'd been a woman. A man. A car seat flying through the air…

Suddenly he remembered all of it. Theresa shouting a final warning at Bill, Bill refusing to back down, then Theresa hurling the infant car seat through the air.

Casey had come out of hiding then, lunging for the awkward plastic carrier and catching it in his arms. Immediately he'd rolled to the ground, using his body weight to cushion the fall, even though he'd already guessed what Bill Voltz had not.

The car seat was empty.

The realization came too late for him. Theresa lost no time in taking advantage of his momentary weakness. She'd raised her gun over his head and that was the last he remembered.

He rubbed the bump that was growing over his left

ear and thanked the Lord that she hadn't decided to shoot him, instead.

Staggering to his feet, he tried to figure out what to do now. Theresa and Bill were both gone. What about Jackie?

He dashed to the street, then stopped and groaned. His car was missing. And the Accord he remembered spotting in front of the school—the Accord he was sure belonged to Theresa—was missing, too.

Only Bill's Audi remained on the street, but all four tires had been slashed.

Oh, God, what was going on? Where was Jackie? And the baby? He reached for his cell phone before remembering he'd tossed it into the back seat of his car rather than return it to his pocket as usual.

He cursed himself bitterly. Where was Jackie now? Was she okay?

And what about the baby?

Running for the nearest house, he wondered what the hell he was going to say to convince the residents to let a stranger with a trail of blood running down his face use their phone at four o'clock in the morning.

JACKIE HIT THE HIGHWAY at full speed and kept accelerating from there. Bill and Theresa were not far behind in Casey's Saab. As she focused on another lane change to pass a slow vehicle, she noticed a distant flash of white that she assumed was the Saab. Faster, Jackie, faster!

Traffic was sporadic this early in the morning,

and that was a bad thing since it made her far too easy to follow. At this point, nothing would make her happier than to be pulled over for speeding and possession of a stolen vehicle. But just her luck, there were no cop cars on the highway right now.

"Haley, sweetie, are you all right?" She still had no idea if the baby was even back there, and if she was, whether she was injured…or worse. She'd decided that her smartest strategy was to take the baby straight to the hospital.

Once Haley had been handed safely over to the medical staff, there'd be time enough to sort out the situation. But the very fact that Bill and Theresa were pursuing her together made her suspect that they had been partners in this all along.

That would explain why Bill still had the three million dollars.

The dirty rotten scumbag. What kind of sick, selfish man staged the kidnapping of his daughter to get some extra dough from his tightwad father?

Jackie forced back a scream as she noticed the flash of white in her rearview mirror again. The Saab was getting way too close. She tightened her grip on the steering wheel and leaned forward slightly. Thank heavens her brothers had been addicted to go-cart racing when she was younger. Remembering all they'd taught her about tight maneuvering and abrupt changes in speed, Jackie waited until she'd passed a van traveling slightly above the speed limit, then pulled into the lane in front of him.

The Saab shot past, shooting out a spray of water

from the wet highway, and Jackie changed lanes again, this time dramatically reducing her speed.

At just that moment, a speeding SUV tried to merge from the right-hand side of the road. Instead of slipping into line behind the van, it raced to pass in front.

"Jeez, buddy! Slow down!"

Tires squealed and Jackie heard the awful, deadly, and all too familiar sound of metal crashing into metal.

Oh, my God. This can't be happening to me again.

But it was.

ON THE BACK OF HIS BMW bike, Casey wheeled out of the station garage and cruised aimlessly through the Courage Bay Emergency Services District. He passed the fire hall, then turned right and circled by city hall, the hospital, and finally back to Madison Avenue.

He'd hoped Jackie would have headed here. But so far he'd seen no trace of his white Saab. He'd put out a bulletin on it and on the Accord, too. But nothing had been reported.

He'd lost about thirty minutes so far. The police unit he'd called first had arrived at the nursery school about ten minutes after the action was over. They'd given him a lift to his own station so he could claim his bike since it was only about half an hour before his shift was slated to begin.

Now he kept listening to the radio, anxious for any news that might lead him to Jackie.

He had no idea what had happened in those precious moments when he'd been lying unconscious outside the nursery school. Had Bill and Theresa somehow abducted Jackie? Or had she managed to get away in time in his Saab?

And what about Haley? Clearly, Theresa had used the infant car seat as a decoy. So where was the baby?

The situation was absolutely intolerable. He was certain Jackie needed his help and it killed him not to be there for her. If she was hurt in any way, he didn't think he would ever forgive himself. The only reason she was embroiled in this mess was because of him. He should have insisted on calling that cab for her...

But she wouldn't have agreed to that plan. He knew it, and still he blamed himself.

The rain was petering out now. Only the occasional fat drop splattered on his bomber jacket.

As he passed the hospital for the third time—still no sign of his Saab or the Accord—finally he heard something from the radio.

"Ten forty-five on PCH heading north. Repeat, 10-45 on PCH."

The words were a ghastly echo from a day not that long ago.

It can't be Jackie. Not so soon after the first time.

Still, he wheeled his bike in the direction of the nearest on-ramp. As he hit his emergency equipment, powering his flashing lights and siren, he prayed that his fears would not be realized.

A pale light glistened in the eastern horizon—a sure sign that the sun would soon be rising.

The first indication Casey had of a problem was the slowing of traffic in the northbound lane. He cut back on his own speed and craned his neck to see ahead. It appeared he'd found the collision. How many vehicles were involved?

He tried to ignore the way his heart hammered at the possibility Jackie might be involved. Again and again he told himself the odds were against it.

On the other hand, his mind argued, if she was driving too fast...if Bill and Theresa were in pursuit...

He slipped out of his lane and onto the shoulder. Zipping past the lines of stalled traffic, he was soon at the scene. Already the problem area had been cordoned off and two officers were directing traffic through the free lanes.

The collision had involved four vehicles. And it looked pretty bad. Behind him he could hear the wailing of approaching ambulances.

Casey parked his bike out of harm's way on the edge of the road. For the first time in his ten-year career, he wasn't able to observe the facts and details of the collision scene with the detached eye of a trained police officer. Instead, he approached the scene as one who knew he had much to lose.

He could hear a woman crying—that might be Jackie. Someone else was moaning with pain. Again, it could be her.

A fellow cop clapped him on the shoulder. "Glad to see you—we could use some help."

It took a few seconds to find his voice. "What happened?"

"A southbound SUV sped up on the approach ramp and ended up merging into a beautiful white Saab convertible. Both those vehicles are totaled. A van and small passenger car were right behind and unable to avoid colliding, as well."

White Saab convertible. He swallowed. "Injuries?"

"We had two in the Saab and one in the SUV. All three need immediate transport to hospital. The people in the van and the small car appear to be okay."

Casey didn't hear anything beyond the fact that there'd been two people in the Saab. Had someone else been in the car with Jackie? Or was it just coincidence that this car was the same make as his own?

Like a sleepwalker, he moved toward the pileup. He could smell motor fluid, burning rubber, the acrid, foul scents of totaled vehicles and damaged people.

He saw a dirty white van with its front end badly crushed. Then he noticed the small car. It was a black Accord, sideswiped, but otherwise not too bad. He paused, and his heart rate accelerated. He circled the vehicle, checked the plates.

It was Theresa Thatcher's, all right.

He glanced in the window. No one inside. In the back seat, a baby carrier had been twisted to the side. It, too, was empty.

Baby carrier. Casey ran his tongue over dry, dry lips.

The SUV was next—overturned like a helpless, crushed beetle. An officer was bent by the driver's door, speaking to whoever was trapped inside.

Casey turned to the final car. The white convertible Saab. He saw at once that it was his. And that it was in very bad shape. There was no one inside, though.

He swiveled, searching for the source of the moans. Not far away he found it—two people lying on the road, a man and a woman, covered with blankets, their injured heads wrapped in makeshift dressings. There was a lot of blood.

Jackie.

He went toward the woman. She had brown hair like Jackie's, and was tossing her head from side to side, moaning, "Help me, help me…"

Oh, God, how could you let this happen?

"Jackie, don't worry, I'm here. Jackie? Can you hear me?"

He'd seen accident victims before, but this was the woman he loved. And he'd only had four days with her.

"Jackie, honey, talk to me. Please."

The injured woman moaned as he kneeled next to her. Then, through the fog of his disbelief and fear, came one clear observation. Jackie's hair wasn't this long. Or this dark.

"Casey?"

He lifted his head and saw her several yards away, next to a patrol car. She was carrying a baby in her arms. Her pants were torn and she had a cut across her cheek, but she was conscious and talking and looking right at him.

"You're okay?" He got to his feet, shaking so badly he could hardly walk toward her. When he was close enough, he touched her cheek and fresh blood dripped onto his finger. Looking down, he saw the one-eyed stare of a tiny baby, who still wore a dressing on her right eye.

Haley.

"She's fine, Casey," Jackie said. "Theresa took good care of her—even the dressing is clean. As for them—"

She nodded toward the couple on the ground—Theresa and Bill, Casey now realized. Why had they been in his car?

"They both have head injuries and a few broken bones, too, but my guess is that they're going to be okay. I made them as comfortable as I could with what I had available. The paramedics are nearly here."

She'd spoken so quickly, he'd been unable to get a word in. Now he wrapped her in a one-armed hug, mindful of the baby between. "What about you, Jackie? Are you all right?"

"I'm not sure how I cut my cheek, but it looks worse than it really is. Other than that, I'm perfectly fine."

Jackie's teeth started chattering. She swayed and Casey had to put out his other arm to prevent her from losing her balance.

She might think she was okay, but he could see that she was in serious shock.

"Come here, honey." He took the baby from Jackie's arms, then walked her toward the ambulance that had just pulled up behind the white van. A paramedic emerged from the driver's door, and something about the tall, brown-haired man made Casey pause.

He's got her eyes.

And then he knew he was meeting Nate Kellison face-to-face for the first time.

CASEY WRAPPED BOTH Jackie and the baby in blankets and settled them in the back seat of one of the squad cars while the paramedics dealt with the more severely injured victims.

Nate had been worried at first at the sight of his sister, but his quick check of her vitals had reassured him. He checked the baby, too, then turned to Casey.

"You must be Casey Guthrie."

"I am." He shook the younger man's hand.

"Isn't this the second collision scene you and my sister have been at in the past week?" Nate looked as if he was expecting a very good explanation.

"It's a long story," Casey said. "We'll fill you in later."

Then Nate had focused on his job, leaving Casey to look after Jackie and the baby, something he was more than happy to do.

One of the patrol officers had a thermos of tea that he offered to Jackie, and the hot liquid seemed to help calm her more than anything else.

Eventually she stopped shaking. Leaning her head against his chest, she said softly, "I want to go home."

"In a minute," he promised. "They've got another ambulance on its way."

"They'll need it for the guy in the SUV. I'm okay, Casey. And Haley needs a clean diaper and a bottle. Can't you get us out of here?"

He considered his options, then grinned. Really, in a way, it was kind of fitting. "I've got my bike," he said, tapping the helmet that he'd only just remembered he was still wearing. "Are you and Haley game?"

CHAPTER SEVENTEEN

THE SUN WAS RISING on Courage Bay, banishing the evening rain. Jackie's arm was wrapped tight around Casey's waist, her face pressed securely to his back. With her other arm, she held Haley in a little nest of blankets that protected her from the cool morning air and the buffeting wind.

Earlier the baby had been fussing, wanting her morning bottle. As soon as she'd heard the purr of the motorcycle, though, she'd calmed. Now she slept peacefully as Casey drove slowly, cautiously, toward the hospital.

This time he did not have his sirens and emergency lights working. The plan was to make a quiet appearance at the ER, get Jackie and the baby checked out, then figure out where to go from there.

Theresa Thatcher and Bill Voltz were already at the hospital, no doubt being seen by the emergency staff. The driver of the white van was fine and had insisted on walking from the scene, but the occupant of the SUV would be transported to the ER by ambulance, too.

Jackie gazed down at the sleeping baby in her

arms. Had any child ever had a more eventful first two months than this one?

She held tight as Casey took the corner that led up to the ER bay. As before, he drove right over the sidewalk to the glass doors. After cutting the engine, he popped the stand, then helped her and the baby inside.

As luck would have it, Izzy was working the front desk again, and she looked at the three of them in disbelief. "Not you guys again."

"We've got to stop meeting like this, Izzy." Casey managed a weak grin before explaining the situation.

Izzy shook her head sadly. "That poor babe. You're sure she's okay?"

"She's fine," Jackie said. "But when she wakes up, she's going to be very hungry."

"I'll get something for her to eat and a clean diaper, too. But first you'd better go talk to that older couple over there." Izzy pointed to the corner of the room. "They're waiting to see their son. They asked if there'd been any mention of a baby. Am I right in assuming…?"

But there was no need to answer her question. Wallace and Abigail had spotted them and were already running forward.

"Haley?" Abigail's face was streaked with tears. She held out her arms and Jackie relinquished the baby to her grandmother.

"Oh, thank God." Wallace wrapped one arm around his wife as he tucked aside a blanket to see his granddaughter's face.

Haley picked that moment to open her one good

eye. She blinked several times, seemed like she might cry, then brightened the entire world with a wide, toothless grin.

Jackie was so glad for the three of them, but without Haley in her arms anymore, she felt…incomplete. She watched the Voltz couple fawn over their grandchild and felt a weary ache in her chest.

"Jackie."

Then Casey's arms were around her and the empty feeling disappeared. He held her close, and in his tight grip she could feel how desperate his worry about her had been.

"I can't believe you're really okay." He closed his eyes. "When I saw the condition of the Saab, I was so sure you'd been badly hurt."

"Sorry about your car, by the way. But I wasn't driving it. I was in the Accord."

"As if I care about the car. But how did you get in the Accord?"

"It's a long story, Casey. Let's sit down, okay?"

He found them two seats, bought her a can of juice from the vending machine, then settled beside her. First she explained how she'd disabled Bill's Audi, then been surprised by Bill and Theresa's sudden appearance and forced to take off with the Accord to save Haley.

Casey recounted all he'd overheard in the exchange between Bill and Theresa, and together they finally put the pieces of the story together.

"What I'm not sure about is whether Sherri-Ann was in on the fake kidnapping scheme or not."

"She was the first time. Only Bill told her he was putting their child in the care of an older woman who used to be his teacher. She didn't know about Theresa at all. When she found out, she was pretty livid."

"What about Rosie? Have you figured out her role in this mess?"

"I think she was helping her sister, but only reluctantly. When the plan fell apart, she tried to do the right thing and return Haley to her grandparents."

"Poor Haley, to have two such dead-beat parents as Bill and Sherri-Ann. Her mother hasn't even shown up to make sure she's okay."

"Sherri-Ann is probably consulting with her attorney as we speak. Let's hope the grandparents end up with custody."

He nodded toward Wallace and Abigail. Wallace had scrounged a bottle of infant formula from Izzy, and Haley, nestled in her grandmother's arms, was going after her breakfast with a fair amount of urgency.

Just observing the scene brought an instant longing to Jackie. She let out a wistful sigh, then glanced up to see Casey watching her with a knowing smile.

"I think I see motherhood in your future, Jackie Kellison."

She smiled and let him pull her close again. He could tease all he wanted. She'd seen the same longing in his eyes, too.

CASEY RANG THE DOORBELL of Jackie's condo. He'd dressed with some care today in a conservative button-up shirt, well-pressed pants and freshly shined shoes. He was out to impress.

Jackie came to the door in a flowered skirt and T-shirt he'd seen her in before. She laughed when she saw him. "Who are you trying to fool?"

"Your brothers."

Kell and his fiancée Melody were hosting a family dinner tonight, and it was to be Casey's first introduction to the Kellison clan. He'd already had a brief meeting with Nate, and had seen Kell at work, and his impression was that once they understood how crazy he was about their sister, they were all going to get along fine.

"Come in for a minute." Jackie tugged on his hand. "We're not supposed to be at the ranch until six."

"Well, all right," he said, pretending reluctance. "Just don't mess up my hair or anything, okay?"

"I'll try to restrain myself." She went to the fridge. "Want a beer?"

"I'd better have a cola."

Again Jackie didn't hide her amusement. "You really are taking this meet-the-family thing seriously."

"You only get one chance to make a good first impression."

"Sorry to tell you this, Case. But you're already on your second impression with my brothers."

"I was afraid of that."

Jackie pulled him to the sofa, then snuggled in close.

"How are you feeling?" he asked her. A couple of weeks had passed since the second car accident, and she'd taken a few days off work to deal with the emotional craziness. They'd been to the police station several times to give statements regarding the kidnapping scheme and Bill, Sherri-Ann and Theresa's involvement.

All three would likely end up spending time in jail. Kidnapping—even when it was your own child—was not a matter taken lightly by the courts.

Permanent custody of Haley had been awarded to Wallace and Abigail, who both insisted Casey and Jackie were welcome to visit as often as they wished.

"I'm fine, Casey. Just so glad Haley is finally safe from her crazy parents and that evil Theresa. Say, did you have any luck in that meeting this morning?"

"I've accepted another retainer," he told her proudly. His decision to hang up his own shingle and run an investigative agency was off to a fast start. Thanks to his contacts in the department, he was well on his way to a successful business.

"Looking for a partner?" she teased. He knew she would never leave nursing.

"Actually, I am," he said. "But not for the agency."

"Oh?" She straightened, realizing he wasn't smiling. This wasn't a joke.

"Jackie, I've known from the first moment I met you that I wanted to spend my life with you. So here's my question. Will you marry me, Jackie Kellison?"

He'd caught her by surprise. As he watched her eyes well up with tears, he started to worry. Moving too fast had been his mistake with her from the start.

"I've blown it, haven't I? You're not ready. You

don't think you know me well enough." He paused. He could tell by Jackie's tortured expression exactly what she was thinking about. "It's Andrew, isn't it? You haven't gotten over what happened…"

One tear spilled from her eye to her cheek. He reached up to brush it away and she caught his hand in hers.

"Can I tell you something, Casey? Something I haven't told anyone else?"

He nodded, all his attention focused on her.

"The day he died, the day Andrew hung himself, he chose to wear the suit he had on when he married me."

Casey tried to make sense of this. "Was it a suit he wore often?"

"No. Andrew preferred casual clothing. As far as I can remember, our wedding was the only occasion I ever saw him in a suit."

"Well, that's strange, I guess." Casey puzzled over why she thought this was important. "Maybe he just figured it was right to wear something…formal."

Jackie gazed down at their entwined hands. "To me it was more than that. I thought that by wearing that suit, Andrew was telling me he'd made a mistake marrying me. That maybe if he hadn't married me, he wouldn't have—"

"Oh, Jackie. No. I can't believe he could have meant that."

She managed a smile. "Well, that's what I believed. For a long time. And I didn't tell anyone because I was so very heartbroken.

"Then, just the other day, I had a thought. I wondered if maybe on the last day of his life, Andrew wanted to remember a time when he was really, truly happy. Maybe he put on that suit and thought about our wedding, and maybe in his very last moments, he was able to conjure up a whisper of the joy that we had on that day."

Casey could hardly speak; his throat felt swollen and his eyes burned. All he could manage was to hold Jackie close. "That's beautiful," he whispered.

"I think so, too. And you know what? It doesn't even matter to me if it's true. It's what I'm choosing to believe."

"That's my Jackie." He wouldn't tell her she was brave and strong anymore. She seemed to always take exception to those words. But he knew they were true. No one could have survived what she'd gone through and emerged as pure of heart and strong of spirit. Those were the qualities that shone through no matter what she did.

"Oh, look what I've done." Jackie pulled back from him with a frown. "I've smudged mascara on your clean cotton shirt."

"You have?" He looked down in horror, expecting to see a big black stain. What would the Kellison men think of him now? They'd figure he'd made their sister cry…

"Kidding." Jackie smiled and tapped his shoulder playfully with her fist. "You're really wound up about meeting my brothers, aren't you?"

"A little," he confessed.

"Well, you're probably right to be worried. Especially now."

"Why especially now?"

"They're prepared to meet my new boyfriend. Not my new fiancé."

Casey froze. Replayed what she'd said in his mind. Smiled. "So you're saying yes?"

"Absolutely. I think I'm going to make the perfect wife for a private investigator. Now, smudge up my makeup for real this time."

To hell with first impressions, Casey decided as he took his bride-to-be in his arms. "With pleasure."

* * * * *

Ordinary people. Extraordinary circumstances.
Meet a new generation of heroes—
the men and women of
Courage Bay Emergency Services.

CODE RED

A new Harlequin continuity series continues
November 2004 with

TOTAL EXPOSURE

by Tori Carrington

Fire Chief Dan Egan pilots a helicopter with Dr. Natalie Giroux aboard to make an emergency lift. A full-blown electrical storm hits. Lightning strikes the chopper. An emergency landing is their only hope....

Here's a preview!

CHAPTER ONE

NATALIE WATCHED AS THE WHITE X of Courage Bay Hospital's landing pad grew farther and farther away beneath them. She'd worked at the hospital for more than ten years, but she'd never seen it from this angle. Through the pounding rain it looked almost surreal.

Who was she kidding? This entire experience had been surreal. She'd never been up in a helicopter before, yet she had helped Fire Chief Dan Egan rescue a stranded victim from his roof moments before the mud slide had claimed the entire house.

A curse filled her ears.

She turned to look at Dan. His right hand was fused to the stick between his powerful legs, his left to a longer one between their seats, which looked like an oversize emergency brake. His right hand and the stick it held shuddered ominously.

"What's wrong?" she asked.

Deep lines bracketed his mouth as he flicked his gaze from the instrument panel, with its seemingly hundreds of dials and switches, to the windshield. "The winds are picking up and I see thunderheads rolling in. The storm's switched course and is circling from behind us."

Natalie looked back over her shoulder. Ominous black clouds pillowed bright, jagged shafts of lightning. She could no longer make out the hospital in the dimming light.

"It's unsafe to try to land back at the hospital," Dan said through the mike. "My best bet is to try to go around the storm and approach the airport from the northwest." He spared her a quick glance, his blue eyes lingering for a moment before shifting back to the instrument panel. "Hold on."

Natalie grasped her harness for dear life as he made a sharp right turn. The wind pushed at the helicopter, causing it to sway in the air.

She closed her eyes and took a deep breath. She'd been so focused on the rescue that she hadn't really stopped to think how dangerous flying in these conditions was. But as the helicopter hit an air pocket and dropped a few yards, she could have sworn her stomach pitched down somewhere in the vicinity of her soaked, boot-clad feet.

Her feet? She suspected her heart had just hit the ground some thousand feet below, lost to her forever. Until it came boomeranging back up with a vengeance and lodged in her throat.

Lightning split the dark sky in front of them, making her jump. This couldn't be safe. Thunder seemed to rattle the windshield of the small aircraft.

Natalie leaned closer to the side window, staring down at the darkness below. Another crack of lightning showed her they were above Courage Bay. The high, churning, foam-capped waves revealed the storm had gone from bad to much, much worse.

She briefly closed her eyes and counted backward from ten. After what she'd seen of Dan and his amazing capabilities today, she wanted to trust him, longed to believe that he would see them through this okay. But this weather, the suddenly very small helicopter, the countless "B" disaster movies she rented to help make the lonely nights go by—all continued to make her the most frightened she'd been since…well, in her entire life.

Another sharp dip. The *whump-whump* of the helicopter blades above them, a loud clap of thunder behind them, the pounding sound of the rain against the windshield and the steady hammering of her heart made her feel as though she was going to be sick.

Another crack of lightning. Only this time it wasn't far off in the distance, but directly in front of them. And just before it disappeared in the dark sky, the nose of the helicopter ran straight into its path.

Dan reached a hand out to cup the back of her neck, then pushed her head between her legs. "Hold on. We're going down…"

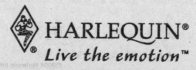

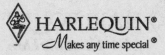

eHARLEQUIN.com

For FREE online reading, visit www.eHarlequin.com now and enjoy:

Online Reads
Read **Daily** and **Weekly** chapters from our Internet-exclusive stories by your favorite authors.

Red-Hot Reads
Turn up the heat with one of our more sensual online stories!

Interactive Novels
Cast your vote to help decide how these stories unfold...then stay tuned!

Quick Reads
For shorter romantic reads, try our collection of Poems, Toasts, & More!

Online Read Library
Miss one of our online reads? Come here to catch up!

Reading Groups
Discuss, share and rave with other community members!

For great reading online,
visit www.eHarlequin.com today!

INTONL